DANGEROUS SECRETS

DANGEROUS SECRETS

ARANDA JAMES

TATE PUBLISHING
AND ENTERPRISES, LLC

Published by Tate Publishing & Enterprises, LLC
127 E. Trade Center Terrace | Mustang, Oklahoma 73064 USA
1.888.361.9473 | www.tatepublishing.com

Tate Publishing is committed to excellence in the publishing industry. The company reflects the philosophy established by the founders, based on Psalm 68:11,
"The Lord gave the word and great was the company of those who published it."

Book design copyright © 2014 by Tate Publishing, LLC. All rights reserved.
Cover design by Joseph Emnace
Interior design by Honeylette Pino

Published in the United States of America

ISBN: 978-1-63063-288-5
1. Fiction / Mystery & Detective / General
2. Fiction / Romance / Suspense
14.01.31

DEDICATION

I would like to dedicate this book to my wonderful parents, grandparents, my sister, my son, and to the man who taught me what it means to be in love, James.

ACKNOWLEDGMENTS

I would like to thank all of the people who helped me with research and answered so many of my questions. I can't thank my family and friends enough for their support. A big thanks to all of the folks at Tate Publishing for working so hard to help make my dream a reality.

PROLOGUE

Light from a bright, full moon shone through the window and lay across the bed. The feminine figure in the bed tossed and turned restlessly. When the moon reached its zenith, it found the woman's dark eyes fixed on the silver picture frame on her nightstand. The picture showed a handsome man sitting in a swing with his arm around a golden-eyed beauty. It captured a moment in time that represented many hours of happiness—a possible lifetime of happiness.

All gone. There was no handsome man anymore. She had sat on that swing yesterday. Alone. Her life had begun and ended with him. She had died with him. She breathed. She existed. But life was gone. The moonlight turned a single tear to a liquid diamond as it slid down her cheek and fell onto the pillow that no longer smelled of soap and man.

Predawn light found Jordyn in the kitchen sipping a cup of coffee. Sleepless nights of pain and loneliness gave way to mornings like this. Everywhere she looked she saw him. His boots were by the door even though she had removed them over a year ago. The small things like the book he was reading or his razor in the vanity had broken her heart at first. Now it was the complete absence of things, the fact that he was becoming a memory. And she didn't want to let go. He was her everything. How was she supposed to let go of everything? She missed the boots, the book, and the razor. She missed him. She wanted him back. She wanted to touch his beloved face and sit in the swing and talk about ridiculous things, talk about life.

She set the coffee cup on the counter before the first sob racked through her throat. Her vision blurred but she could still see the images in her mind. The image in her heart was just as clear. She didn't hear the birds singing outside her window. She didn't see the beautiful sunrise. Noon found her curled up on the couch wrapped in a well-worn flannel shirt whose sleeves fell way below her fingertips.

CHAPTER 1

Six months later.

"Come on, Jordyn. You promised you'd go with us." Faith Blanchard's voice was as whiny as it was when they were kids, and Jordyn didn't want to do something Faith wouldn't do on her own. "It won't kill you to get all dressed up and go out. And it's for a good cause. Tell her, Mon." Faith turned her baby blues on Monica Wallace. She was as worldly as Faith was sheltered and her dark green eyes usually reflected this fact, but right now they were sparkling with the possibility of getting their bereaved friend off of her land and into town.

"Jordyn, you know we both love you and we are concerned for you and we really want you to go." She said this with all of the sincerity of a matron. Jordyn was not fooled by the act. She rolled her eyes and looked from one to the other.

"You both know that the 'we're-concerned-about-you-therefore-you-should-go-to relieve-us' routine won't work on me. I'm an expert at dodging this particular strategy. Furthermore, you both know that although I'm not planning on dating in the near future, I'm fine and getting on with my life." She sighed and extended her hands with a shrug as if coming to some conclusion, "Therefore, there's some other reason you want me to go to this charity auction and I'm not even going to consider it until you tell me why." With this statement, Jordyn flopped onto her couch and folded her arms expectantly, eyebrows raised.

"You refuse to go without a better reason, huh?" Mon asked. Jordyn's answer was to cock her head slightly, arching one eyebrow.

"Well, if you don't go I'm going to buy the most evil-looking bachelor there and send him on a date with Faith." Monica said this with the superb confidence of someone who knew they had just won a serious argument. Jordyn looked at Monica incredulously but Monica met her gaze head on. She was serious and Jordyn knew it.

"Why is it so important that I go?" She had already prepared herself to give into their wheedling because there was no way she was letting Faith go out with an unknown man who allowed himself to be auctioned, even if it was for a good cause.

Monica sighed heavily. "We told you that we just really think you should get out."

"Yeah," Faith chimed in.

Jordyn looked at her two friends with many, many questions wandering around in her head. Oh, well. She would find out at the auction. She smiled and said, "Guess what? I don't have a thing to wear so I suggest that we go shopping before tomorrow night or I'm going to be out of style."

In nearby Knoxville, TN, Monica and Faith proved their eagerness to help her shop for a dress…and then shoes. And then things she definitely didn't need, but she had so much fun buying them and spending the day with her friends that she didn't mind. Jordyn smiled and laughed as they shopped the stores. When they were eating their lunch in an excellent Italian restaurant, she smiled as she realized that she had come a long way in the past six months. And it was mostly thanks to Monica and Faith, her two gorgeous friends. Jordyn almost laughed on several occasions as practically every male server tripped over themselves to bring something to their table. On top of having silky black hair that fell to her waist and the clearest green eyes Jordyn had ever seen, Monica was tall—in fact, very tall. Monica had always thought that her almost six feet in height was damaging to her feminine appeal, but if the waiters were any indication, her height wasn't a problem at all.

Jordyn's eyes roved to Faith who was smiling at a very over anxious waiter as he refilled her water glass. Faith was the ultimate Barbie doll—blonde hair, blue eyes, and perfect figure. But the best part about Faith was that she wasn't vain about her beauty and frequently lamented her looks in comparison with her friends. They had been friends since they were sent to the same boarding school one year and discovered that they had lived close to one another all of their lives. As she listened to the animated talk flowing around and to her, Jordyn couldn't remember when she had been without these two wonderful friends. They had been dubbed the Three Musketeers, the Three Stooges, and a variety of other trio clichés throughout their teens. Now they were just the best of friends.

Jordyn raised her water glass, "To friendship and trust."

CHAPTER 2

The three women arrived fashionably late to the charity auction intended to raise money for a variety of environmental research projects. The auction had been geared to appeal to the very rich women of the very best families. The money would go to fund research grants for environmental studies focused on issues and species in Tennessee. Jordyn wondered if any of the proceeds would end up funding research programs that would involve Promise Land, her family's twenty-thousand-acre conservation farm. Her grandfather had set the farm aside when he had become more than comfortably wealthy. He insisted that it was what his grandfather would have wanted. The older gentleman had always insisted that God wanted him to be a good steward of the land and he had biblical evidence to prove it. Generations later, his family was still upholding his idea. As they ate their dinner, the three discussed people and projects there that Jordyn had lost touch with.

Monica looked across at Jordyn. "You're having a good time, aren't you?"

Jordyn smiled easily. "I am. This is turning into a very good evening and you guys get the credit for it. But I have to admit that I'm still curious as to why I absolutely had to come. When do I get to know?"

"Do we have to have a reason? An ulterior motive? Maybe we just wanted to spend an evening among the rich and richer and we wanted you with us." Faith's answer was a bit too quick to be taken seriously.

"You haven't taught this girl how to lie well yet," Jordyn said wryly to Monica.

"I'm working on it," Monica answered blithely, as if teaching lying was an everyday activity for her.

Jordyn put both hands on the table. "Well, while you two are deliberating on whatever plans you have, I'm going to walk around in the gardens before the auction starts."

Jordyn left the ballroom by one of the many glass doors strategically placed all around the semicircular room. The patio was wide and wrapped around the ballroom with huge columns supporting the high ceiling. There were occasional steps that lead off into the extensive gardens that fanned out in a star-like design from the patio of the ballroom. She wandered far enough from the diners for the voices to be lost in the songs of the evening birds.

Jordyn couldn't help but feel more at home outside of the ballroom than inside, not that the ballroom wasn't spectacular. It was gorgeously decorated with extravagant centerpieces for each table set for a formal dinner. The room was lit with what seemed like a thousand candles and strategic lighting to give it an opulent ambience. The orchestra had been replaced by an oldies band, currently crooning to the ladies about new love, getting them in the mood for bidding. It had been a pleasant evening, but she wasn't used to all of the activity. She was appreciating the quiet when she sensed someone walk up behind her. She turned around to see a tall man in a well-fitting tux. His hair was either black or very dark brown and it glinted with health. He took a step closer to her and said, "Hi."

Jordyn let her lips curve into a courteous smile and nodded. He smiled a bit hesitantly and extended his hand. "My name is Braeden Parker and I will confess to following you out here on purpose."

Jordyn's eyebrows rose at that. She didn't think the face was that of a psychopath, but you never could tell these days. "Can I help you with something?" Her voice was cool, making it clear she didn't really want to help him with anything. She tilted her head slightly as she waited for his response.

Braeden Parker felt like he had been sucker punched. He had seen pictures but her eyes were much more intense than any picture could show. Beautiful was a common description of the heiress to the Grey fortune. He looked hard at her and decided that she clearly deserved that title, but he would have called her striking, traffic stopping, or maybe even beautifully unique. Ice princess was another term and at the moment she was justifying that title as well. She was only about an inch shorter than his height of five feet nine inches. She was slender, but not thin. She looked feminine but also athletic. And her black formal gown only gave subtle hints at the curves beneath. For some reason, her modest dress made him less nervous.

Braeden realized how long he had been silent and his eyes flew to hers. The reaction at his obvious appreciation for her showed in the eyes now dancing with amusement. Eyes that had went from gold to a light golden brown and demanded an answer. "I would like to conduct a follow-up study on your property." He blurted it out and then stopped as he realized how unexpected that must have sounded and then waited for the instant denial.

Jordyn watched the man with interest. More interest than she had had in anything in the past year and a half. He was... intriguing. The tux clung to broad shoulders and tapered down to slim muscular hips. He had nice legs. Not too long, not too short. His eyes gave her the feeling that he could be trusted. That was important to Jordyn.

"Why?" Jordyn asked.

"Well, I was involved in reintroducing the red wolves onto your property two years ago. I would like to see how they're doing." He said it all in one breath and expected her to immediately say no.

"And why are *you* asking to do a study *now*? If I recall correctly, the scheduled evaluation is supposed to start at the first of next spring, not this spring. And Dr. Marcy has been working on the project."

Braeden hesitated a moment before answering. "I was a graduate student of Dr. Marcy's and I'm still working with her. I currently teach at the same university and I'm taking some time off to work on some pet projects. No pun intended. I wanted to start a little early so I can have more time to collect and evaluate data and then develop a new plan if needed. She told me if I had your approval and the funding to go for it." He shrugged. "I've got the funding."

Jordyn took a step closer to the ballroom windows. Braeden followed. "I actually received your formal request in the mail today, but I haven't had a chance to look over it. Can you tell me a little about the specifics of your study?"

Braeden's face relaxed into a smile as he thought about his life's work. "Well, many of the wolves now present do not have tags or GPS collars. I want to capture and tag as many as possible. I would like to collar as many as I can as well as set out trail cameras on popular hunting routes. Essentially, I want to do some home range analysis and population dynamics stuff." He paused a moment and then went on. "I realize you don't normally have room for extra researchers, and that's not a problem. I can sleep outside if I have too, as long as I have a dry place to store my equipment and work." He ended with a bit of a rush and Jordyn couldn't help but smile a little. He had slipped his hands in his pockets as he had talked and the relaxed pose was contradicted by the excitement in his voice when he talked about his work. As he had talked, they had drifted closer to the window. Light flooded the patio and Jordyn really looked at Braeden Parker. He had dark brown hair with gold highlights probably added by the sun. His face was tan and his eyes were the most brilliant blue she had ever seen. His nose was straight and his Cupid's bow mouth looked very kissable. Her thoughts startled her. She hadn't felt attracted to a man since…in a very long time.

Despite her sudden hesitation, his excitement about his project made her decide that she would make a call and possibly rearrange the schedule a bit. Dr. Hayes would probably be glad to have the extra preparation time for her study of newts. She needed more help anyway. If Dr. Hayes seemed okay with the new arrangement, Jordyn would talk to Braeden Parker after the auction and tell him that if he started soon, he could stake his claim on the much-desired property for the next year.

Braeden watched Jordyn closely as she considered his request. He desperately wanted her to agree to the change in schedule, but he had tried to hide that desperation. He was still a little off balance at meeting her. Her silky, deep red hair combined with eyes that could only be called gold stirred him in a way he didn't want to admit. She was both sure of herself and seemingly vulnerable at the same time. The combination was fascinating at the least and devastating if dwelled upon. He stopped his train of thought before he got off track. He wasn't here to gawk at the beautiful and enticing Ms. Grey.

Her ice princess look stayed in place as she spoke, "I'll consider the possibility of the change and check the schedule. I'll let you know after the auction. You will be here, won't you?"

"Yes, and thank you," Braeden said on a sigh of relief, looking directly into those eyes.

"Don't thank me yet, Mr. Parker. Enjoy your evening," Jordyn said this as she walked away. Parker plowed his hand through his hair as he started walking around to a side door. She wasn't what he would call an approachable person. He'd know if he could go on with his plans after this ridiculous auction. He still couldn't believe he'd had to be in the crazy thing. It was for a good cause, but still. As he went backstage to prepare for the slaughter, he couldn't help but let his mind wonder back to Ms. Grey and the real reason for his premature presence.

Jordyn called herself every kind of fool when she walked away from Braeden Parker. She had stood there and appreciated all of the maleness and enjoyed his assessment of her. She had let a weird attraction allow her to say she might rearrange an entire year's schedule at a moment's notice. Attraction was the only word for what she had felt when she looked into his eyes. Eyes that she was sure would change color with his mood. Her steps slowed as the last two years came screeching into her mind. She remembered a different pair of eyes. She remembered another mouth that had given her gentle kisses on a rainy afternoon that had turned the evening to passion. She had forgotten all about Tommy and she hated herself for it.

As she rejoined Faith and Mon after a long phone conversation with Dr. Hayes and a few others, including the Tennessee game folks, she vowed never to let her thoughts wonder to places they shouldn't go. Monica looked at Jordyn's set face and asked, "Who was the hunk?"

Jordyn knew where the question had the potential to go and she felt too disconcerted to go there. "Braeden Parker. He's a wildlife biologist."

Monica knew that a wildlife biologist equaled a business acquaintance which meant Jordyn would never get involved with him. Finding Jordyn a nice date as well as a legitimate excuse to go on the date had been the reason she and Faith had pushed so hard to get Jordyn here. Still, a biologist was a business acquaintance and Jordyn had used the excuse before.

However, Monica had seen Jordyn's reaction to the man as she unashamedly spied through a window and now saw the business angle for the excuse it was. She had gotten in the habit of letting Jordyn get away with lame excuses because she knew how much Jordyn still grieved for Tommy. Tonight however, she had watched from the dining room as Jordyn responded to a man for the first time since Tommy, and she had made up her mind that Jordyn needed a push in the right direction. Preferably without tipping Jordyn off that the whole reason for dragging her here tonight was, in fact, to get her a date.

"He's very appealing. I wish I had some business acquaintances that looked like that."

Jordyn didn't rise to the bait. She told them the basics about his predicament hoping that it would satisfy, but Monica wasn't ready to let it go so easily.

"Guys like him don't come along very often. Why don't you get to know him, invite him out to dinner and see where a moonlit stroll might lead?"

Jordyn turned her gaze from the ornate ballroom and met Monica's eyes. Monica's suggestion was very close to Jordyn's own thoughts. The pain and confusion in Jordyn's eyes struck Monica far more than Jordyn's quick, "I will as soon as you mind your own business." The tone was playful, but the point was clear.

Monica stayed quiet because she was hoping that the confusion might be a result of the encounter with the handsome man. Faith patted Jordyn's hand and said, "She's sorry. We just hate to see you so…" her words trailed off as she looked to Mon for help, "unhappy," she finally finished.

Monica took a long sip of her drink and looked at Jordyn. "You're not unhappy. You're miserable. It's like you're sleep walking through your life." Monica reached out and squeezed Jordyn's icy hand. "Honey, I know you still love him, but Tommy wouldn't want you to live the rest of your life alone and unhappy any more than you would want him to. He'd want you to let go and get on with the business of living."

Quick tears filled Jordyn's eyes at the serious words. She knew Monica was right. Trust her to pull no punches and speak bluntly about the matter. But she was right. Tommy wouldn't want her living like this. Even though she appreciated Mon's uncharacteristically caring and sincere words, it still hurt.

"I don't know if Braeden Parker is someone you need to get to know better but you need to find out. If it's not him then maybe someone else. The point is you have to give life a chance. Promise me that you'll try to live a little." Monica was rarely so serious for such a long period of time.

Jordyn returned the pressure from both their hands before she smiled at them. "I don't know what I'd do without you two."

"Well, you wouldn't have anyone to watch your back or make you do things you didn't want to do, even if it's for your own good. We're priceless, that's for sure." Monica leaned back and looked around. "And it's a good thing we are here for you because here comes, Angela." Monica's words were said with a large pasted-on smile. Angela Beaumont had always been jealous and catty toward Jordyn.

"Hello, Jordy!" Angela's sugar sweet voice grated on Jordyn's nerves. Faith smiled uncertainly as Angela approached. Monica settled back ready to jump in with both claws. Jordyn hated the nickname Jordy and Angela knew it. Tonight however, she wasn't feeling like dealing with Angela's pettiness.

"Angie dear, how are you?" Jordyn nodded slightly while looking over her shoulder. At the nickname, Angela's eyes narrowed. Angela had always hated being called Angie. She thought it made her sound less rich and distinguished. Angie got the point and tried a different tact.

"Here to buy some companionship?" Her tone had turned a bit nasty and just as Monica was getting ready to jump in, Jordyn suddenly smiled. It was the million-watt smile that she had once used to dazzle the press into publicizing only what she wanted them to.

"Not particularly." Her tone was so honey-smooth that Monica almost laughed as she finished with, "I'm here to see who else has to resort to this."

Jordyn said it in such an innocent, naïve way that Angela blinked, unsure if it was a slam.

"Well, I'm here because it's my social responsibility." With this, Angela turned and walked prissily away.

"She knows she never has and never will hold a candle to you and it kills her."

Both Jordyn and Monica turned to stare at Faith. It was rare that she said anything negative about an individual. Just as Monica opened her mouth to tease the angelic Faith, the lights went dim everywhere except on stage. A spotlight hit the auctioneer and the fun began.

The linen-covered tables had been set up in a semicircle around the ballroom, with its focal point being the stage that was backed up to the largest exit curtain. A stage on which the bachelors were to show off had been erected with a short runway that jutted out within two feet of the closest table. Jordyn had to laugh at the antics of the bachelors, most of whom had been railroaded into being here. And she had to blush at the complete lack of manners demonstrated by the supposedly well-bred women. The second to last bachelor was called up. Jordyn was stunned to see Braeden Parker walk onto the stage. She had assumed he was involved in organizing the event, not as part of the attraction. He was smiling but clearly wishing he was somewhere else. He spun as directed and took the tux jacket off and slung it over his shoulder at the demands of the raucous front tables. As the bidding began, it quickly became evident that he was a favorite.

Monica leaned over and said, "Your Mr. Parker might get the high price tonight."

Jordyn was quick to say, "He's not my Mr. Parker." However, Monica noticed that she said this without turning her eyes from him. Jordyn barely heard Faith's soft "Uh-oh" when she heard the bid start at the highest bid of the evening.

Every eye in the ballroom turned to Angela Beaumont. It was typical of her. She was acquiring the best-looking bachelor with the highest bid of the evening in the most public way possible. Jordyn's eyes swung back to the stage where her eyes met Braeden's. He was begging her with those eyes. She knew it just as clearly as if he had shouted, "Help!" Without realizing what she was doing she called out a higher bid.

A shocked hush was followed by a low wave of feminine voices. Well, now everyone knew Jordyn was out and about. Angela shot her a murderous look before calling out again to the auctioneer.

"Get 'em, girl!" Monica encouraged softly. Faith was almost bouncing out of her seat with excitement. Jordyn didn't notice anyone else. All she was watching were Braeden's eyes.

She increased her bid and though she said it quietly, everyone heard her. Angela practically screamed her increased bid. In the same quiet voice as before Jordyn took the bid higher once again. Angela had risen but as if suddenly realizing the spectacle she was making of herself, she sat down. Jordyn won bachelor no. 26 with the highest bid ever at this particular charity event. She didn't notice how everyone looked at her approvingly. She didn't consider whether they were glad she was moving in society again or if they were just glad someone had bested the youngest Beaumont brat.

"Whew," Faith said, "when you decide to make a statement you really go all out!"

Jordyn smiled a little. "No one is more surprised than me."

"Well, intended or not you caused a stir." Monica's voice was low as she asked, "Do you want to slip out?"

Jordyn's emphatic, "Yes!" made Monica and Faith move quickly to get out of the ballroom. As they headed toward the front door calling farewells, they gave one another secret, victorious smiles. Operation Jordyn Dating was one step closer to being accomplished.

Monica wasn't the least bit worried about what was getting ready to happen. She had done it before and would probably do it again. This time, however, she was doing it for a friend instead of an irresponsible older sister. The tall good-looking man that walked in didn't scare her. He was supposed to, that much was clear. The piercing eyes were slate grey. The dark blonde hair was cut in a military style and the suit was typical for the FBI. And he didn't have a clue what he was up against. As he folded himself into the seat across from her and fixed her with a stare, she almost smiled. If he only knew how unimpressed she was.

"You wanted to talk to me?" His voice was cold and indifferent. He clearly was there simply because he was being forced into this meeting.

"Why are you following Jordyn?" Monica got directly to the point. Her question made one of the man's eyebrows quirk upward.

"Is that any of your business?" His voice and manner implied that he had no intention of answering her question. He probably considered her a spoiled rich kid whose daddy had political connections that she played with when she was bored. Or maybe he thought she enjoyed power. She sighed inwardly. Either way he'd be wrong.

"Yes, it's my business. Jordyn Grey is a very close friend of mine who has been through a lot and I don't want her to suffer more because of your ineptitude." She fixed him with a hard stare that tended to work on an adversary's confidence. He didn't seem phased. She leaned a little closer across the table. "She saw you twice last week. So far, she doesn't know who Tommy was or why he was there. If you keep showing up, she's going to wonder why and if she wonders then she'll worry. She has a very untainted view of Tommy and I want to keep it that way." Monica stopped and took a breath. She was getting angry and that wasn't good. Oh, how she hated this situation! She folded her arms and studied the man for a moment. "If she spots you again or if you make her life uncomfortable in any way, you'll answer to me."

Monica's tone hadn't changed at all through the entire conversation. However, as she had talked about Jordyn, the man across from her had noticed her eyes soften and when she had delivered the threat, he had noticed how cold they had become and how sincere that threat was. Maybe she wasn't the spoiled rich kid whose daddy had political connections she considered her own personal toys for when she was bored. Something about her wasn't right for that. He knew they had tons of "agents" who were not in any computer system or in any file. He had a feeling the illustrious Monica Wallace was not what he had first thought. He made the quick decision to cooperate…for now.

"She saw the tail?"

Monica suddenly felt very tired. She was way too close to this situation. "Yes, she called me Monday after her trip to the grocery store and Thursday after a trip to the library. She joked that she obviously hadn't been out enough because she felt like somebody was watching her. If she senses you're there, you're a bit too close."

"Agreed. The agent is a newbie and a bit overzealous at times." His voice wasn't apologetic, just matter of fact.

Monica sat back in her chair and crossed her arms in a confident manner that only added to her beauty. He noticed. "Look, I'm providing you with an impeccable schedule on her. You don't have to stick to her like cheap perfume. I'm pretty sure she doesn't know anything or she would have told me by now."

The man's look was thoughtful. This rich girl genuinely cared about her friend. That was great for her image but bad for an agent. It could get her killed someday.

"Ms. Wallace, I'm sorry that you feel we are not doing our jobs correctly. I will do my best to make our presence more subtle. I appreciate that you feel Jordyn Grey doesn't know anything, but

I think she may know more than you think. She may not even realize she knows something important." He paused to reflect on what he was about to say. "Furthermore, you need to be aware that we are not the only ones watching her. One of my agents is pretty sure someone else was following her last week, as well. If they think she knows something, then the chances are she does."

He felt the weight that fell on Monica at that reminder. She didn't respond and her face was showing a bit more strain than it had when he had first walked in.

"I thought this would be over when Tommy died, but in a way it's worse. At least they were only gunning for him last time." She looked him square in the eye and he suddenly felt the impact of those deep green eyes. They made him think of a lagoon. He could get lost in those eyes. He couldn't help but wonder if they grew darker when filled with love. That thought made him blink.

"Do you really think he told her anything?"

The man shrugged one shoulder. "I doubt it knowing Tommy, but you never know. They got a lot closer than we had expected. They got married, didn't they? If he did tell her something, we need to know as soon as possible. It would make life easier on everybody, especially Ms. Grey."

Monica nodded but her mind was already leaping ahead to the next morning. She was going to Jordyn's for the day. She was going to have to push a bit harder to see if Jordyn knew Tommy was in the witness protection program and why. The fact that Jordyn had been one of her best friends for most of her life made the job harder in her eyes although her superiors considered it her greatest strength. The man cleared his throat and Monica turned her attention back to him.

"I'll let you know the minute I find out for sure if she knows anything."

"I'll try to make our presence less felt."

The words were clearly forced through a mouth that was not used to backing down for anything or anybody. Monica smiled.

This man was clearly used to getting his way, not compromising. "I wasn't the spoiled brat you thought, was I?" When he didn't respond Monica continued, "I bet you hate being wrong about someone."

The man smiled for the first time. Monica was taken aback by the intense liking she had for that smile. Wow, she needed to get away for a while. This situation was getting to her.

"I will admit to having certain preconceived notions about what you would be like and that they were partially wrong. However, I'm still not convinced that you know what you're doing."

His words zapped the warmth his smile had given her. "Guess what? You're wrong again. I may have been born with the proverbial silver spoon in my mouth but I'm *very, very* good at what I do."

He cocked a questioning eyebrow. "You may be good but you're too close to this case. The very fact that you're working it seems like bad judgment to me."

Monica's voice held no small amount of sarcasm. "Well, I'm glad you're here now to take up the slack." She stood and gathered her purse and threw her cape around her shoulders. When she looked up he had also stood and she could look him dead straight in his arrogant albeit handsome face. His tolerant expression made her mad. Without considering what she was doing, she reached for his hand and practically dragged him outside.

When they reached the sidewalk she stopped abruptly and turned on him. "There are two men inside the coffee house who have to be with you. One is in his mid to late thirties and is wearing a blue suit and white shirt. The other is in his early twenties, wearing khakis and a polo. Looks like a computer geek. The minivan over there has at least two more of your people in it. One female, one male. The female is about five feet seven inches with light brown hair. The male is trying really hard to look like you but he's about ten years younger." She raked her eyes up and down him. "From the stiff, offended attitude you have I would guess that you've spent the last few years behind a desk. What's the matter? Did you anger the wrong people? You drove a blue Cadillac here, you were driving a jeep Cherokee yesterday, and a white Ford pickup the day before that. *You* have been following *me* ever since you arrived last week and you really stink at it. You may not like me, my pedigree, or this situation but you have no right to question my ability to do my job *so back off!*"

With those words, Monica turned and stalked to her car. She got in and as the engine of her bright red Porsche roared to life she said, "I meant what I said. Bother Jordyn again and you'll pay. Maybe with your job." She enunciated this by spinning gravel at him as she exited the parking lot.

He smiled as he watched her go and flexed the hand that tingled from her not-too-gentle touch. She had spunk all right. His boss had said if anybody could pull this assignment off, it was Monica. He had doubted it at the time. But that was before he met her. As he headed to his car, he couldn't help but wonder if Monica's breathing fire at him at every turn would be an all bad experience.

Monica fumed as she drove away. The nerve of that upstart! If anybody didn't know their job, it was him. Jordyn had spotted him or one of his unit! Well, she would just have to take care of this little problem because apparently she was the only one who could. Despite being handsome and having a killer smile, this guy couldn't get the job done. She should call her superior about him but she didn't want to unless absolutely necessary. This situation was proving to be more complicated than she had ever thought it would be.

On the ride home, Jordyn had trouble reasoning her behavior at the auction. What had caused her to act so out of character and actually buy a date? She suddenly remembered Tommy goading her into pushing her new sports car to outrun a local deputy.

She had later apologized to the deputy who had very sternly written a ticket based on her confession and then told her it had been a good experience chasing the car. At the time, it had been exhilarating, even dangerously appealing. And completely out of character for her. Now, she felt she was doing something similar and it scared her to death. It scared her for reasons she didn't want to identify or examine.

If she were honest with herself, she knew that she was reacting to Braeden Parker. Something about him pushed her outside of her norm. Not to a dangerous or reckless action like Tommy, but in a way that made her act outside of her box. She felt disloyal to Tommy for the reaction Braeden Parker elicited from her. They hadn't been married long, and as Monica frequently pointed out, a six-week marriage didn't warrant Jordyn's lifetime devotion. Jordyn always got the impression that Mon knew something about Tommy that she strongly disapproved of, and she had definitely been against their relationship. However, Monica had never said a word about him after their elopement. Still, it was the undercurrent of disapproval that kept Jordyn quiet regarding the truth about her and Tommy.

Jordyn sighed heavily. She was tired of the intricacies of her life. She was still working on moving on with her life, but it was working on her nerves. She had even started imagining people were watching her. If that didn't prove she was in a tangled emotional state she didn't know what would; because nobody had a reason to be following her around.

On impulse, she pulled to the side of the road and let the top down on her convertible. She pulled back onto the road and headed toward a favorite spot. She drove to the top of Christmas Hill and enjoyed the view. She could see what looked like millions of lights from Pigeon Forge and Gatlinburg on one side and beautiful mountain silhouettes backlit by what seemed a million stars on the other. She hadn't been here since the first time she had brought Tommy. She had been trying to show him her deep attachment to the place. He'd been bored with the stars, the view. He'd ended up kissing her until she was way past breathless. They had gone home and spent their last Saturday night together. The memory brought a bittersweet smile, but no tears. She was finally healing.

CHAPTER 3

Braeden Parker couldn't believe his good luck. She had agreed to his request for an early study and offered a place for him to stay. Much to his surprise, she had called him after the auction with apologies for rushing out before she had a chance to speak with him. She had pulled his file for his phone number and seemed very interested in getting the project started. She asked about his lodging plans and when he had told her he was planning on staying in town and driving to the farm every day, she had offered the use of an apartment over one of the barns, built to accommodate researchers and fortunately empty. Over the next couple of days, they had talked frequently by phone as arrangements were made. So, he was going to be staying on her land and he had a date with her. The new set of circumstances would definitely make life easier for him.

He tried to make himself believe that he wasn't excited about spending time with a beautiful and intriguing woman and staying on her farm, which few people had even seen. He tried to ignore the fact that she had caught and held his attention from the moment they had met. He'd felt like an idiot during the bidding, until her eyes had met his. She had worn her wealth and status well. She had come across as one aware of the privilege and responsibility of power. She had won the bid without seeming overly excited or upset. In fact, she had almost seemed bored she had been so matter-of-fact. He'd been dreading the bidding for him until he'd caught sight of her. He'd wanted her to bid. A date with her would make what he had to do easier, but it was more than that. He'd desperately wanted her to bid and win just because he wanted the woman he was interested in to be interested in him. When he looked into her eyes, he had known the attraction he'd felt was mutual. He'd also seen her pain and confusion. If he could, he would be honest with her. He would tell her what he was there for and how he felt. Two days after the auction, it was as impossible to tell her the truth as it had ever been.

"Lord, help me get through this without hurting either of us." The prayer was short and specific, but desperate.

At six thirty, he was standing on Jordyn's doorstep, truly shocked at how little security the place had. The gate where he had been prepared to use the intercom had swung open automatically when his truck tripped the sensor. He shook his head at how vulnerable that made the property.

He rang the doorbell twice. After several moments with no response, he knocked loudly on the door, expecting a butler to answer. A slow smile spread across his face at the variety of noises that eventually began to emanate from inside. Evidently, there was no butler and it sounded like Jordyn was fighting a small war to get to the door.

The knocking in Jordyn's dream ended up being the real thing. She spun on her side to get up and landed on the floor. Oh right, she had slept in the living room last night. She struggled to her feet and stumbled into the coffee table, yowling loudly as she grabbed her shin.

"This had better be good Fai—!" She was yelling as she finally flung the door open. And just stared.

Braeden was doing some staring of his own. If he had thought Jordyn gorgeous at the auction, nothing could have prepared him for the beautiful if rumpled woman before him now. The oversized flannel shirt swallowed her. Her hair was falling over her right eye, begging to be brushed back. Her eyes, or eye, looked a bit confused and disoriented. Her right shin sported a bright red streak and the toes of her right foot were digging into the luxurious rug covering the rock floor of the foyer. His eyes went back to hers when she pushed her hair back. The smile on his face wasn't deterred by the scowl on hers. She looked too adorable to pull off the ice princess.

Jordyn was mortified. Faith had told her she would be here at six to cook her breakfast because today was the anniversary of her first date with Tommy. She had told her not to come, but had assumed it was Faith when someone knocked. She was usually up before now but she had been out until four with one of the mares who was going to be a mommy for the first time. She was definitely looking her worst. She had taken a shower and landed on the couch for a short nap. She could only imagine what he must be thinking. She was admittedly envious of his neat appearance. His somewhat shaggy hair was still damp from a shower and he looked clean and masculine in well-worn jeans and a charcoal grey pullover. She opted for sarcasm as the best defense.

"It's a little early for a romantic date, don't you think?" she asked, completely forgetting about their business arrangement and his scheduled arrival this morning.

Braeden realized she was still half asleep and decided to tease her a bit. "That depends on your idea of a romantic date." He waggled his eyebrows suggestively and said, "Some people think watching the sunrise together is a very romantic date."

"Well, it's not my idea of a romantic date." She was decidedly grouchy in the mornings.

Braeden adopted a hurt little boy look. "I'm sorry to hear that. It's my favorite time of day."

Jordyn was a bit more awake now and said a bit saucily, "Mine's sunset. Come back then." Then she shut the door.

Braeden would have been offended if he hadn't seen the amusement dancing in her now alert eyes before she shut the door. He knocked again.

The door opened and her eyebrows were raised in question.

"I'm actually here about the passionate objective of my life. There are more wolves out there than ever before and I'm real anxious to go make their acquaintance."

Jordyn smiled at his description of his job. He wasn't thinking of the brutally hard work, but the benefits of it. She laughed easily and gestured to one of the barns closest to the house. "You can unload your stuff into any of the offices there. We have wireless internet so you can check e-mail if you like. The password is lobo20. I'll be there in a minute."

She closed the door on his nod and listened to his fading, booted footsteps. She had been befuddled by his appearance. That was how she explained her teasing him. She was absolutely *not* flirting. As she dressed, she couldn't help but think about how good the bantering had felt.

Braeden unloaded his gear, which included two hundred digital trail cameras, before Jordyn put in an appearance. He was admiring the house, the barns, and the land that surrounded them. They weren't ostentatious, but elegant and functional. The driveway was marked by four huge pillars and two wrought iron gates. The drive was a two-lane affair with willow trees on both sides and down the middle of the grass median. The drive entered a yard area and circled in front of the house. To get out, one had to pass by the huge barns sitting opposite of the house before continuing on the exit side of the huge driveway.

The house was a one-story sprawling home that ran east to west. It had cathedral ceilings, skylights, huge windows, multiple fireplaces, and a porch that seemed to wrap around the entire house, with doors leading onto it from each room on the outside wall of the house and sporadic steps leading to the grounds. It was well kept and had a homey air, despite its size. Braeden smiled at the swing lazily swaying in the breeze, dangling from chains fixed to the porch, and the melodious notes of the windchimes hanging by the front door. The driveway loop provided an empty space in front of the house that had been filled with a huge fountain. The fountain had a statue of a horse, a war horse by the look of it, tossing a flowing mane, nostrils flared. The water spouts were sending gallons of sparkling water into the early morning light and filling the air with the musical sound of falling water.

As he looked around, Braeden couldn't help but smile as he noticed a log cabin and two large barns in a field on the west side of the house. If he were a betting man (which he wasn't), he would say that the log cabin was kept there as a reminder of where the Grey family had come from. Everything seemed to be perfect, right down to the horses silhouetted by the morning sun. Even the two huge barns and low slung bunkhouse looked well cared for. He smiled as he turned a full circle. No matter his reasons for being there, he was going to enjoy this place.

Jordyn strolled up to him, smiling at his reaction to her home. "It's truly beautiful, isn't it?" She hadn't asked it with the arrogance of ownership. Instead she was admiring the view the sun was making of the rolling hills, mountains, and elegant horses.

"Beautiful," Braeden responded. The splendor of the land and its buildings were forgotten. He was watching the sun bathe her face in a pale light that lent her an angelic glow.

"How did you end up here?" Realizing how that question probably sounded he quickly added, "I don't mean to be intrusive or insulting, I just have a hard time picturing someone like you being happy here." He flushed a little as he dug himself in deeper. "The place is beautiful and the house is as nice as any you would find in the Hamptons, but it's so far from…anywhere." He finally just stopped talking.

Jordyn shrugged and shot him a smile that showed she wasn't at all offended by his question. She decided to give him the short version as they walked into the barn. "I always loved this place.

Even as a child, I would rather come here than anywhere on earth. When I married, Dad gave me this house instead of one closer to a city." She gestured to the fields backed up to rolling hills and then steep mountains. "He knew I'd be happier here." He'd also thought that would make Tommy settle a little better, but she didn't mention that. "I have three full time employees who help me keep the place up so I have plenty of time to work with the researchers on the farm. We keep horses for the trails the electric buggies can't go on, so feel free to use them anytime."

Braeden wondered at her mention of her marriage and then the smooth transition to the help and horses. Did she do that to avoid questions?

After *ooohing* and *ahhing* over the amount of equipment he was using, she settled him into one of the many small apartments over the barn and gave him the key. "It's fully equipped with a stove, fridge, washer, and dryer. And I took the liberty of putting a few groceries in the fridge and in the pantry."

She stopped at the door to the tack room and looked him full in the face. "I hope you enjoy your stay. I'll see you around noon to introduce you to the hands and show you around the farm."

A stab of guilt pierced him at how sincere she had been. As he made his way with his gear up to the nicest apartment he'd ever stayed in while doing research, he saw her riding away on one of the trails she had pointed out. The horse was beautiful and the picture of grace horse and rider presented was breathtaking. He sighed as he realized that he was beginning to admire Jordyn Grey for more than her beauty. He hadn't anticipated a genuinely nice, likeable person.

Jordyn may have presented a picture of grace, but her thoughts at that moment were tumbling all over one another. Two days ago, she had received a call from Rafe, a local bodyshop owner. After Tommy's death in the hit-and-run, she hadn't wanted to even see the car again. She had sold it to Rafe. She didn't even know when it was released from the police impound once the investigation stalled out. Rafe's call brought back a lot of unwated memories and a lot of questions. After exchanging pleasantries, Rafe had hesitantly asked, "I hate to bring it up, Jordyn, but did you keep anything of value in Tommy's car?"

Jordyn's response was quick, "No, why do you ask?"

Rafe cleared his throat before answering, "I thought you might want to know the car was released from the impound last week and I have it here at the shop."

"That's fine, Rafe. The car *is* yours. I'm not interested in buying it back." And she hoped to never see it again.

"That's not exactly the problem. This morning when I came in to start working on it, I discovered that it had been *thoroughly* searched."

"I don't understand," Jordyn hated even thinking about the car.

"The seats were sliced, the trunk lining was ripped out, even the console was torn apart. It wasn't like that when I picked it up, somebody searched it last night." He paused before venturing, "It was probably some riff-raff looking for something they could steal out of a fancy car. I just thought you might want to know."

"I'm sure you're right, Rafe. Was anything taken?"

"Not that I can tell."

"Good. It was probably just a fluke, but thanks for letting me know though."

Two days later and she was still thinking about the call. By itself the car being searched wasn't a problem. It was just the latest in a growing list of odditites. No matter how hard she tried, she couldn't seem to figure out what all of it meant. She couldn't shake the feeling that they were all connected to Tommy and it was all important. She just couldn't make sense out of any of it.

She smiled a bit as she turned down a trail that would lead horse and rider back to the barn where Dr. Parker was waiting. Maybe Braeden's study would be a welcome distraction from her complicated situation.

After stowing his gear and being introduced to the three hands, they headed out. Braeden had never met such characters as her hands before. If the place had a foreman, Dave would be it. He was the eldest of the three and obviously the boss, next to Jordyn of course. His face was lined with years of hard work and sunshine. Although the man was clearly getting on in years, he still looked as tough as old rawhide. He didn't like Braeden and made no secret of it as he barely gave him a nod. The horse he had been riding seemed to move on without a word or move from his master.

Corey was probably the second in command and was as devoted to the farm and the Grey family as Dave was. He was tall and thin. His black hair was liberally sprinkled with grey, but his eyes were quick to smile. His sunny personality seemed a direct contradiction to the more cantankerous Dave. Braeden smiled at the thought of the two men working together. Corey was a talker, there was no doubt about it. Jordyn had found him in the barn fixing a loose hinge, talking away to one of the cats. "We're goin' ground hog huntin' this evenin'. I'd say you'd like that, wouldn't you, Velma?"

When he spotted Jordyn, his eyes lit with pleasure. "Good morning, Miss Jordyn."

Jordyn's smile was full of genuine caring and liking for the man. "G'morning, Corey. I want you to meet Braeden Parker. He's the one doing the wolf study."

In contradiction to Dave, Corey held out his hand with a smile. "Welcome."

Braeden shook the offered hand. "Thank you."

Jordyn indicated Corey with a small lift of her hand. "He knows this farm as well as anyone and he'll be a big help for finding the best places the wolves like and frequent."

Braeden nodded and smiled at the man as he said, "I do like to keep an eye on them if I can. As much as folks don't like it, they have more of a right to be here than cattle or horses."

Braeden agreed as Jordyn asked the man where Neal was. "He's chopping wood." The old man chuckled. "He was none too happy with the job but Dave insisted. He'll be a good hand someday if he lives through Dave's training."

Jordyn was smiling as they left the barn. "Dave trained Corey so I guess Corey's getting a kick out of watching Dave break in a new hand."

"How old is Dave?" Braeden asked.

Jordyn shrugged. "He was old when I was a little girl. I can't ever remember him not having grey hair and wrinkles."

Braeden laughed softly at the description. He continued to ask questions about the farm and its operations as they headed toward a small shed with an awning attached to the back. Braeden could hear the steady whack of the axe biting into wood before they came into view of the young man swinging it.

Neal was barely sixteen and clearly taking out his frustration at Dave on the logs he was splitting. Jordyn wisely waited until the axe head was buried deep in a poplar log before calling to him.

"Good morning, Neal!"

The young man turned and immediately the scowl that marred his handsome young face disappeared. Braeden instantly recognized the adoration for Jordyn that shimmered in the young man's eyes. A glance at Jordyn showed that she knew it as well.

"Dave has you working the wood pile again does he?" Jordyn's voice was warm but not overly so.

"He says I need to build some muscle. He doesn't seem to realize that I was one of the best fighters the Blades ever had." The young man's voice was full of pride at this last statement.

Jordyn shook her head. "Fighting doesn't mean you're strong, Neal. I'd say most of those gangsters wouldn't last a day in the world a hundred years ago."

At Neal's look of disappointment that she hadn't been impressed at his boast, Jordyn smiled. "Keep at the wood. Dave can teach you things about living that no gang will ever understand."

Neal nodded. Braeden wasn't certain if Jordyn's words had really sunk in, but he somehow felt that over time the continual reminders might make a difference for the boy. Neal's eyes had already found and assessed Braeden as a rival. "Who's he?"

Jordyn frowned at the boy's lack of manners. "This is Dr. Braeden Parker. He's here to do a wolf study."

The boy squeezed Braeden's hand in what was supposed to be a hard grip. Braeden smiled. "Pleased to meet you, Neal."

The boy dropped his hand and asked, "You going to be here long?"

"At least 'til the end of the summer."

Neal nodded with obvious dislike. "Always takes you guys a long time."

"Well, we try to be thorough."

Jordyn spoke up, "We are all going to give him our complete cooperation. If he needs something, help him."

Neal nodded as he looked at Jordyn like a besotted puppy.

As they walked away Braeden said teasingly, "I'm glad you were there or I might have ended up like some of those poplar logs."

Jordyn shook her head. "He's incorrigible, but he's better than he used to be." She smiled easily as she said, "He wouldn't hurt you."

"I don't know about that. I got the feeling that if I had touched you he would have chopped my hand off."

Jordyn laughed at that description. "He's a bit…infatuated with me."

"That's an understatement." Braeden glanced at Jordyn curiously. "How'd you end up with an ex-gangster on Promise Land?"

Jordyn sighed. "He's the grandson of one of Dad's oldest and dearest friends. He got caught robbing a convenience store about a year ago. They were going to send him to a juvenile delinquent center and Dad called me. The farm was a lifesaver for Neal, just like it was for me." Jordyn gestured to the surrounding fields

DANGEROUS SECRETS

and forest. "As you can see, there's not a lot a young man miles from town and no car can get into out here. He does school work in the evening, which Corey oversees and he does farm work during the day. And I'm sure you've noticed that Dave is a pretty hard taskmaster."

"Neal really doesn't look like a gangster," Braeden commented with some confusion. "How does a farm boy end up like that?"

"You should have seen him when he got here," Jordyn chuckled at the memory. "Dave took one look at the boy and told him to go change into clothes that fit."

Braeden smiled at that. "I'd say that didn't go over well."

"It didn't. Neal told Dave to make him. Five minutes later, Neal was outfitted in jeans, a work shirt, and boots. He's never really bucked Dave since. He just watched when Dave burned his ever present bandana and handed him a baseball cap. I think he has a good chance of reforming and making something out of himself."

"Thanks to people like you and Dave. I know a lot of folks who wouldn't have bothered." Braeden sighed at his thoughts. As if her beauty wasn't enough to get him in trouble, she was caring as well.

As they jostled along in one of the buggies used at Promise Land for how unobtrusive their electric motors were to the wildlife, Jordyn studied her newest resident with interest.

"What made you choose wildlife biology?" She asked quizzically.

Braeden smiled at the question and gave the answer that normally surprised people. "Mostly my family."

Jordyn gave him a sidelong glance as she kept the buggy on the trail.

"I think that's going to need a little explanation." She paused as she maneuvered around a large puddle, waiting for Braeden to answer.

"When I was a little boy, I always enjoyed hearing the stories of my family's struggles with living on the land. My grandparents had what we call a hillside farm. During the Depression, my grandfather lost his job in a coal mine and they did everything they could to survive. The farm didn't provide enough to eat and they turned to the land. Deer, bear, raccoon, and even opossum were on their menu." Braeden hesitated, trying to find the words to make Jordyn understand. "I've heard stories passed down to my father and to his father about specific animals they encountered. There was one wily old 'coon that they could never trap. As they began to depend on the world around them, they began to see how much the world around them also depended on them. Other people were depending on wild animals for their meals as well and the animals started disappearing. After the Depression, my grandfather was one of the biggest fans of trying to conserve the wildlife in our area. I guess it was a tip of his hat to the animals that sustained him." Braden smiled as he continued his story. "One story that has been passed down and possibly embellished involves a black bear that my grandfather hunted for weeks. One evening, my grandfather was on a cliff, watching the sunset after a fruitless day of hunting. The story goes that he glanced over his shoulder and there stood that big ole bear. The bear looked at my grandfather and then at the sunset before sitting down and watching much as my grandfather had been doing." Braeden grinned at Jordyn. "He never did harvest that bear. They say that my grandmother accused him of developing a soft spot for it because he thought that bear was enjoying the sunset too."

"And these stories made you develop a love for the land and the animals that inhabit it." At Braeden's nod she asked, "When did you figure out that you wanted a wildlife biology degree?"

Braeden was surprised at her easy understanding of and interest in the origin of his career. "In my second year of college, I discovered a class that fit perfectly into my sleeping schedule. It didn't start until twelve-thirty." He paused at her light chuckle. "The class was Principles of Fisheries and Wildlife Biology.

I changed majors the second week of the course and I've been hooked ever since."

"And how long did it take to get your Ph.D.?"

Braeden chuckled lightly as he remembered the days when he thought he would never get his dissertation finished. "Eight and a half years"—Braeden smiled fondly at his memories—"which is better than the average but still felt like an eternity at times. I won't tell you that I loved every minute of it, but I love what I do."

"It's important to love your life's work." Jordyn's voice sounded sad and reflective. He wondered if she regretted leaving the Grey Foundation.

"Don't you enjoy running the conservation program here?"

Jordyn's face lit up. "I love it. I've been hands on for about two years, but I've always loved this place and what it does." She glanced at him as she added, "I minored in wildlife biology."

"Really?" Braeden feigned surprise. He'd read about her education in a newspaper bio.

Jordyn nodded. "I loved every minute of it. But a degree in communication was best considering I was earmarked to be the family's hand in the foundation." She paused and then asked, "How did you pick red wolves for your dissertation?"

Braeden noticed the smooth change of subject, but laughed as he responded. "I love predators."

Jordyn laughed along with him. "I'm sure that has nothing to do with family stories."

Braeden shook his head, still smiling. "Oh, of course not." After making sure she knew he was kidding he continued, "My grandfather used to tell stories of mountain lions. Even though science disagrees with him, he claims to have seen a wolf one time when he was a boy."

"Do you believe he did?"

Braeden thought before he answered, "I think he did. Dad says he described the eyes as intelligent, golden, somehow knowing. And he was a Godly man, lying would be totally against everything he knew. And he claims he didn't tell anybody about it at the time."

"What was his reasoning for that?" Jordyn thought she knew, but she wanted to hear Braeden's explanation.

"Predators are feared. The only reason we still have foxes is because they're so small. I guess it runs in the family to feel that we should treat the land with the respect and care that its Creator did." Braeden shrugged. "He tried to do his small part to protect the world he knew even then was swiftly disappearing."

Jordyn smiled. "That sounds a lot like my grandfather and his reasons for establishing Promise Land."

Braeden smiled ruefully. "It's too bad that there wasn't as much knowledge about wildlife at the beginning of the nineteenth century."

Jordyn laughed at his expression. "I take it you moan over what could be."

"I do to a certain extent. We'll never see buffalo as they once were, but the world as they knew it was going to change whether they were there or not."

"So how does all of this lead to your current career?"

Braeden continued with his story. "Well, we are now seeing whitetail deer populations at record highs due to conservation. We see mule deer populations coming back. Almost every deer species is now a conservation success story. Even elk, like in the Cataloochee Valley, North Carolina, eastern Kentucky, and Buchanan County, Virginia." His look was intense as he said, "The only animals we still fight are predators. Wolves send ranchers into oblivion. Coyotes are hated despite the service they perform aiding in keeping deer populations from spiraling out of control. Even bears, which are more omnivores, not carnivores, are feared." Braeden turned slightly to face her and gestured as he warmed to his subject. "You see, people tend to only want the animals they feel safe or comfortable with to be successful at surviving. People like deer, unless they're in their gardens."

Jordyn gave a light laugh. "I guess that's true. You always hear about ways to repel deer and other critters from gardens."

"It will continue to be a problem because deer populations are on the rise. Contrary to popular perception, there are more woods now than there has ever been. More habitat equals more deer and now there are also fewer predators." Braeden smiled a little. "Most people don't realize that there used to be wolves, a subspecies of elk, and woodland bison in the southeastern United States. And that's only to name a few. Their environment changed and with that change, the animals and the methods for dealing with the animals have had to change."

"I realize that there are many species now extinct or pushed west and are no longer in this part of the country, but now that you mention it, most of the animals totally removed are predators."

Braeden was impressed by Jordyn's grasp of the situation. "Actually, records show that there are fewer predators in Virginia now than when settlers ate venison at the first Thanksgiving. And we have seen some of the damage this can cause. Fewer predators and more deer equal overpopulation. Natural predators such as wolves and mountain lions and the occasional bear are not present." Braeden shook his head in obvious regret at the situation. "Furthermore, they have very little chance of populating their old hunting grounds once again because of public opinion."

"So how did this all lead you to red wolves?" Jordyn asked again.

He shot her a self-deprecating grin. "I got a bit off track, didn't I? It must be the teacher in me. I decided I wanted to be a conservation police officer and I was for a while. I loved my job, but felt I wasn't doing enough. I was going to college at the same time, trying to get my degree. I told you about the wildlife class." At Jordyn's nod he continued, "I decided I wanted to see if there could ever again be a balance between natural predators and their prey." Braeden shrugged. "We, the human population, have changed the environment so much that at this point it would be a disaster to just let nature take its course. We've changed nature too much for that to happen."

"So you became a conservationist instead of a preservationist?"

He grinned. "Sort of."

"Enter red wolves…" Jordyn's voice trailed off.

"Exactly. Red wolves are one of the ways that we can conserve a species as much as possible. Obviously, the world will never be the same, but as we gain knowledge of the ecosystems of our planet, we can do something about conserving it as best as we can. Sort of stopping our damage and repairing as much as possible."

"That's why places like Promise Land are great for introducing predator species. Red wolves are great because they're not as big as grey wolves. People aren't very keen on having wolves and mountain lions share their backyard, so the smaller the predator, the better their chances of surviving in a world that fears big, toothy grins." He looked at Jordyn as she pulled the buggy to a stop next to a large sycamore as wide as a small truck. "You already have an excellent deer management program in place. A few natural predators might just let us see how close to a balance we can get in our modern world."

Jordyn had listened and now asked an intelligent question, "I thought wolves only went after fawns? Won't that be a problem?"

Braeden shook his head. "No, a pack can take down a mature buck and frequently do so. They mostly prey on older or injured animals and extremely young animals. As we know, fawns aren't helpless for long so that leaves the older and injured animals at the top of the menu. In essence, they ensure the quality of the herd by picking out the weakest individuals. They will prey on some fawns, but they shouldn't have an adverse effect on the herd."

"As our herd health and nutrition has increased so have our fawns. We almost always see two fawns to each doe. We are seeing triplets much more frequently and every now and then we see quintuplets. The former manager told me that it was going to be a problem eventually."

"I imagine it's hard to run a farm like this and trying to reintroduce predators."

"You're not kidding. Luckily, there's more sympathy for predators than ever. At least in this area."

"Well, the wolves should help their own image as time goes by. Times have changed and fewer people have their living depend on their stock. Hopefully, they will be seen for the wonderful creature they are."

Jordyn looked at him with respect. "They are rather incredible. Do you think they will ever be able to repopulate all of their previous territory?"

Braeden's look was thoughtful but he didn't hesitate in answering. "No, not in today's modern world. There are cities and towns where they once lived. I do think they might gain a foothold in more rural areas though. At least, I hope they can. It's been a dream of mine for quite a while to help these guys spread out a little. I have a feeling that once people start seeing them in a nonthreatening way, they'll be a bit more accepting."

Braeden noticed her smiling at his rather intense speech. "I'm not saying that everything about the predators is good, just that there's more good than bad." He shrugged, defending his not so well thought of view of animals.

"I couldn't agree more. That's one of the reasons my grandfather established this place, giving the animals that aren't so popular a chance."

As Jordyn pulled several maps of the farm, including a topographical map, out of a map pouch to show him the boundaries, he couldn't help but look forward to the coming weeks. He was looking forward to spending them with a woman like none he'd ever met before. She not only listened to his ideas, but understood him and why he thought the way he did. That was a dangerously attractive combo.

Jordyn and Braeden bounced along the borders of Promise Land for a whole day and a half. Braeden was surprised that there was a good clean trail along the fence between Promise Land and its bordering properties. One of the reasons the property had been chosen for the release in the first place was the fact that it was bordered on two sides by the Great Smoky Mountains National Park. But there was a good fence even on those two borders for the most part. At one spot between Promise Land and the Park, the fence had been cut and clumsily spliced. Jordyn noticed and pointed it out. They decided to cross the fence and check out the surrounding area. They hit a park service road of sorts in about a quarter of a mile from the fence with car tire tracks. Jordyn frowned, "I wonder who could be up here driving a car. You would need a four-wheel drive if it was wet."

"Teenagers?" Braeden suggested.

Jordyn shrugged, "I'll call the park service tomorrow and tell them to keep an eye out. There's a locked gate at the entrance of most of their service roads and nobody but one of the rangers or forest service personnel should be on those roads anyway."

As they headed back to the buggy, Jordyn couldn't shake the uneasy feeling the spliced fence gave her. A few nights ago, she had the unwelcome sensation that someone was watching her make the rounds to close up for the night. She had comforted herself with the knowledge that there was no access to the property except through the main gate. A few weeks ago, on a rare trip into Knoxville, she had thought somebody was following her too. She had chalked both up to her frazzled emotional state over the past two years, but now she began to wonder. What would someone want with her or Promise Land that would warrant a long and uncomfortable drive up that service road? Did this have anything to do with Tommy's searched car?

Jordyn was lost in thought as they trudged the short distance back to the buggy and headed out. Braeden stayed quiet, waiting for her to voice her thoughts and trying very hard to interpret what the spliced fence and fresh car tracks might mean to Jordyn. She appeared worried and slightly afraid. Braeden didn't know her well enough to say if her reaction was normal or if something she might know would cause the unusual concern.

Back on Promise Land, and not far from one of the main ponds on the property, they came upon Dave, Corey, and Neal repairing the fence and cleaning brush out of it.

Jordyn smiled warmly at them, with no trace of her previous pensive moments apparent to her hands. "I think ya'll look like you need a break."

Dave shoved his hat back and smiled easily at Jordyn before his eyes swung to evaluate Braeden. For some reason, Braeden felt he should scoot a little farther away from Jordyn.

"I think a break sounds like a fine idea." Dave's eyes twinkled as he asked, "Is there any reason in particular we should break now?"

Braeden noticed that both Corey and Neal were grinning from ear to ear and were heading to their vehicle, rolling up their sleeves as if to wash their hands. His eyes swung back to Jordyn who wore a particularly innocent expression and was answering Dave's question.

"Oh no, I just want to make sure my hands don't work themselves to death."

Corey and Neal had reached the Buggy and were looking at Jordyn like expectant three year-olds, smiling. Jordyn sighed dramatically, "I suppose you want some kind of treat for all of the hard work you're doing."

She climbed out of the buggy and began rummaging in the back, coming up shortly with a container. When she lifted the lid, the most heavenly chocolate smell made the mouths of all men present begin to water. Dave, Corey, and Neal all took a large muffin bulging with nuts and chocolate chunks.

"It's as delicious as ever, Jordyn," Corey's mouth was full but his words were distinguishable.

Jordyn smiled as she passed the container to Braeden who gratefully took one. He'd been wondering if he would have to wrestle for one. And after he took a bite, he decided that wrestling for one would have been worth it.

His amazement showed in his rounded eyes as he said around a mouthful of chocolate goodness, "These are phenomenal!"

Jordyn laughed delightedly as the four men quickly demolished a dozen muffins and looked longingly at the empty container. Dave, Corey, and Neal washed them down with large gulps of water before Dave turned to Jordyn, "If you have a minute, I'd like to show you a few things I think we need to either change or at least keep an eye on."

Jordyn's eyes swung to Braeden. "Do you mind?"

Braeden shook his head. "Not at all. You go ahead."

With Braeden's assurance that he was okay with losing a little time, Jordyn and Dave headed out in the buggy. Braeden moved to the fence where Corey and Neal were replacing a few posts that had been broken by a small rock slide from the cliff above.

"Can I help?" Braeden asked.

Neal shot him a doubtful look. "Have you ever dug post holes or strung fence?"

"Once or twice," Braeden replied evenly.

"Well," Corey interjected, "we need all of the help we can get. I like Jordyn's muffins but I would still like to be home in time for Neal to cook a decent dinner."

"I was hoping you guys might forget about that," was Neal's sheepish response.

Corey laughed loudly and then explained. "Neal made his brags that he can cook and so Dave and I are giving him the chance to prove it tonight." He winked at Braeden, "We think it might help cure his desire to brag on skills he might not have."

Braeden moved to take a turn at wrestling the broken end of the post out of the ground, enjoying the banter. A few minutes later, Corey decided to check out the cliff and see just how stable the rocks there were. "No good repairing a fence that's going to get demolished with the next cloudburst."

Braeden and Neal worked in silence until Braeden spoke up, "Do you know what you're going to cook?"

Neal looked like he might make a smart aleck comment before he sighed and said honestly, "I have no idea. I'm not sure I can even boil water."

Braeden nodded. "Well, I've got to go to town for a few things this evening. How about you and I go to the store? I know of a recipe that I think you might could handle and it should impress your tormentors."

"Why?" Neal questioned suspiciously.

Braeden grunted as he lifted another post and dropped it into the whole. "Because I know how it feels to be the young guy around a bunch of older guys and needing to prove yourself. What do you say?"

The corners of Neal's mouth tilted up, almost smiling at Braeden. "It sounds like a great plan to me. What am I going to cook?"

Braeden started to explain and then fell quiet as Corey moved into view. He couldn't help but smile as Neal returned Corey's teasing about his cooking ability, or lack thereof, with confident ease. He hoped this worked out.

CHAPTER 4

The next morning found Jordyn and Braeden working with topographical maps, aerial maps, and GPS equipment. They were trying to plan the best locations for the trail cameras. They were working in the large office of the barn where the maps were spread over the sidewalls of the room. The front of the large room had two large screens. The desks along the walls were lined with computers and printers. The room looked more like a state-of-the-art classroom than a research office.

Jordyn stood next to a map with twenty or so red dots in varying locations. Each dot indicated the location of a red wolf that had been previously released. They had been released in areas of the farm that had been deemed good wolf habitat.

"These will probably be good places to start. Twenty wolves of our current population were tagged, so I would start with those. Each radio telemetry frequency is in the file on each wolf, as well as all previous data." At Braeden's nod that he had the files she asked, "They've been here for over two years now. Is your main focus to change their batteries?"

Braeden shook his head. "I have several goals I hope to accomplish with this project, a minor one is to change the batteries so we can keep getting daily GPS coordinates."

Jordyn nodded thoughtfully. "What exactly do you need to accomplish your many goals?"

Braeden smiled at how intensely she was attacking this project. The guy managing Promise Land during the original release was no slouch, but Jordyn was clearly more invested.

"First, I need to get as many animals collared as I possibly can. The National Science Foundation funded the research on their reintroduction and they are funding my project for an update. They are keeping close tabs on the wolves."

Jordyn shrugged. "They want to keep a close eye on their investment here. If we're successful then they will fund it in another location."

Braeden nodded. "Something like that."

"So, if we accomplish nothing else we need to collar as many animals as possible."

"Correct." Braeden ploughed a hand through his hair as he continued, making the hair look disheveled and the man look like a little boy. "Also, by tagging we will be able to get population density estimates. With the cameras and GPS data, we will be able to pinpoint where their home range is in order to determine how much they range in adjacent properties."

Braeden picked up a smooth, green, plastic box and smiled. He had a truly gorgeous smile. "This is a Nature's Eye. It's a video camera that operates day or night. It's tripped by an infrared sensor and can be set to record for different lengths of time. It was developed for hunters, but it has proven to be an invaluable research tool. It doesn't flash like a camera, so it doesn't scare off the animals. It has been very useful in studying lions, cheetahs, jaguars, pumas or mountain lions, deer, and wolves." He had slipped into the voice one would find in a commercial and he ended with a flourish of the camera and a big smile.

Jordyn shook her head at how much he resembled a little boy holding up a prized toy. "You like the Nature's Eye, I take it?" She asked dryly.

All innocence Braeden asked, "How can you tell?"

Laughing, Jordyn asked, "How many do you have? We need to make sure we have good locations for them."

Braeden frowned in disappointment. "They're around $1,000 a piece." He shrugged. "I could only swing six of them." He clearly thought that six was not enough. Jordyn wondered if six really wasn't enough or if the devoted researcher in him just liked them better.

Braeden studied the map and said, "I want to put the Nature's Eyes at fence crossings on the border of your property. It usually takes animals a while to cross under or over a fence. I'll hopefully get some good footage."

He opened another box and rubbed his hands together enthusiastically. "I also have a little over two hundred digital trail cameras. They're basically the same as the Nature's Eye but they take still pictures instead of video and some of them flash. I should have a ton of pretty pictures before I leave. I had a student researcher have a bear practically licking one and we got some interesting tooth pictures."

Jordyn smiled at his exuberance. She had to admit that it was contagious. She found herself smiling back at him. "How are the cameras going to help you find out about deer/wolf interaction?"

"I'll be getting plenty of deer data along with all of the wolf data. I'll have to do some habitat evaluation also. You know, evaluating canopy cover, species and overall health of trees, green floor vegetation, and stuff like that."

"There's always a little work before you can really have fun, isn't there?" Braeden smiled and continued, "By the end of the study, I'll have a pretty good idea of what's out there. I'll compare the deer density estimate with the one they did B.W., before the wolves, and I'll look at the data from the last habitat evaluation. A comparison of the two and," he spread his hands wide and said triumphantly, "then I'll know if wolves could keep deer populations from spiraling out of control even in such a controlled environment."

He shrugged as if what he planned to do was simple. Jordyn shook her head. "That's all, huh?" Her tone implied that she couldn't believe the research was even worth the time. Her small smile and head shake had given her away though.

Braeden nodded. "I know it's going to be a lot of work. But as soon as we figure out where the cameras need to be, I'll set them out. It'll probably take a couple of days just to set them out.

Jordyn pointed to two spots on the topo map. "Here and here are good spots for two of the Nature's Eyes. I'm pretty sure that both the wolves and the deer are crossing the fence here."

"Great," Braeden smiled. "Two down, two hundred and four to go." He pointed to some fields. Once we get the cameras set up, we will start livetrapping and tagging the wolves along the field edges."

"How do you plan to do that?" Jordyn was doubtful that even Braeden with all of his gadgets could get the shy creatures anywhere near an open field.

"I ask them," Braeden said so matter-of-factly that Jordyn blinked.

"You ask them," She repeated slowly.

"Sure," he answered easily, "if you ask them nicely they will come right to you."

"And how do you do that pray tell?" Her question and tone clearly portrayed her doubt.

"You don't think I can do it?" He smiled smugly. "Well, the laugh's going to be on you. I'll show you once we get these cameras out."

"We?" Jordyn asked.

"Well, if you're going to do the fun stuff like livetrapping then you have to help with the rest too."

Braeden's heart was pounding. He didn't know if he wanted to spend time with her. No, he definitely wanted to spend time with her. He just felt guilty for his reasons. No, his reasons were good. *He* really did want to spend time with her. But he did have a job to do as well. And it was what he was supposed to do that was making him feel guilty and hopeful all at the same time.

"Are you trying to bribe me to help you?" Jordyn tilted her head to one side.

"No, not exactly. But findin' out how to get the wolves to come and visit is valuable information that took years to accumulate. I can't go givin' it away for free." He was cute when he adopted the good ol' Virginia boy accent.

Jordyn looked at him seriously. "Do you really want the help? I had planned to help you set up the cameras just to make sure you didn't get lost, but I can help you with anything else you need." She shrugged. "You're the only researcher here and I've got some time."

Braeden felt like she had punched him. He felt like the lowest thing to crawl the earth. He was taking advantage of her. Every time he pushed for a little and she gave him such sincere generosity, it made him want to hit something. He swallowed hard, tamping down the sick feeling in his gut.

He frowned as he studied her. "I really could use the help, but it would be nice if I had someone stronger. I don't think your pretty face, as beautiful as it is, would impress upon those wolves to lie still and let me tag 'em." He shook his head in contemplation, seeming to look her over. "Still, you do have some experience and you're offering to help. I guess you'll do."

Jordyn's face had turned slightly pink at his comments. "Then I guess I need to start helping sort the cameras then."

Braeden fished in a box and came up with a camera. "Do you know how this thing works?"

Hours later, after sorting and organizing SD cards and batteries and getting each camera ready for the woods, they decided on the general areas to place them. Jordyn told Dave where they were headed, and then she and Braeden set out to take care of a few cameras. After only a few hours, Jordyn was having a hard time thinking of this as work. She was having way too much fun to call it work.

Braeden Parker was a walking encyclopedia of useful information and useless facts. She was willing to bet he was dynamite in the classroom, but she got the impression that he would prefer to be in the field. He took care of the equipment even though it didn't belong to him. The grant was set up so that the equipment purchased was the property of the university. He took the time to show her exactly why he set cameras a certain way at a certain place. He was easygoing and determined at the same time. He cared about what he did.

Later, as she was carefully packing cameras in large totes for Braeden to load onto the buggy for the next morning, she couldn't help but consider him as a person worthy of her admiration and respect. Especially after her talk with Dave where he had explained how Neal had returned from the store and cooked manicotti that was quite delicious. Both Dave and Corey suspected that Neal had a little help with the meal. Jordyn decided to find out.

"I hear you have a great manicotti recipe," she said casually.

Braeden was surprised at the comment, but kept his features schooled. "Where did you hear that?"

"Dave mentioned that Neal cooked him and Corey a good meal that wasn't burnt or tasteless." Her look told him he was caught.

He laughed a little uncomfortably. "Don't give me more credit than I deserve. All I did was help him buy the ingredients and give him the recipe. He did all of the rest." He looked up at Jordyn and said seriously, "He really wanted to impress those two and not just because he had made his brags. He told me that if it weren't for them and you, he'd either be dead or in prison now. It did him good to be able to give a little back."

"You're a good man to help him out, Braeden Parker," Jordyn said softly.

He stopped mentally congratulating himself for getting that much closer to winning her trust when Jordyn asked, "So you can cook as well as set fence and catch wolves. Do you have any other secret's Braeden Parker?"

Braeden smiled a little weakly and didn't know what to say. Braeden was thinking of himself as the lowest of the low. He was lower than snail sludge. When they were kids, Bailey, his little sister, had told him he was snail sludge for teasing her about being a tomboy. She would be even more disappointed in him now. He'd used Jordyn's kindness against her. The guilty knot in his stomach prevented him from accepting the drink she offered or carrying on the conversation. He'd manipulated a wonderful human being in order to gain her trust. And eventually betray it.

His silence caused Jordyn to say, "I'm beat. I think I'm going to turn in. What time should I be here in the morning?"

"Around six should be fine. You can't set cameras in the dark although it is easier to hack out trails in the cool of the morning. You might want to wear snake chaps if you've got them. A machete wouldn't be a bad idea either. I'll take water and snacks although I hope to be back here by lunch for another load of cameras."

He was talking as Jordyn made her way toward the door smiling and nodding. "And I should wear the most comfortable hiking boots I own." Jordyn was still smiling as she headed out the door. "See ya tomorrow."

Braeden smiled at the spot where she had been standing. Guilty feelings or not, he intended to enjoy Jordyn Grey's company.

CHAPTER 5

The next few weeks settled into a routine. They met in the barn and took care of trail cameras, batteries, and data. Jordyn helped Braeden set and maintain the cameras. He frequently sent her to check one quadrant while he went to another. The total of two hundred cameras allowed for one hundred camera sites since cameras were set on both sides of a trail. Still, it was time consuming for only two people to tackle checking them all twice a week. They would go over the pictures in the evening after downloading them onto jump drives and Jordyn found that she enjoyed both the work and the results. She was a hands-on owner after all. Braeden had discovered from Dave, the reticent foreman, that Jordyn herself was helping fund a project on newts. That fit with what he was coming to know about Jordyn. In the file he had read on her, he had found that she was in charge of the Grey Foundation, the charitable organization for the vast family fortune. Since Tommy's entrance into her life, she had become less and less involved with the running of the foundation. She had also dropped off of the social radar not long after she and Tommy started dating. The fact that Tommy tried to keep low key didn't surprise him. But he had been surprised that Tommy and Jordyn had worked on the place themselves. He'd been under the impression that the farm and house was fully staffed. When he'd mentioned the lack of help to Corey, he told him that Jordyn hadn't kept on the extra staff after Tommy died. Only Ava would come to clean once a week.

Everything he'd learned about Jordyn Grey contradicted the spoiled picture he'd had of her. There was more to Jordyn than met the eye. Her courtship and six-week marriage to Tommy had changed her from the innocent, giving socialite to the more subdued, tragedy-touched woman she was now. There were times she was so pensive, he worried about what she might know. She hadn't said anything suspicious and he was having a hard time deciphering if her unease was normal, or if there was another cause besides Tommy's death.

Braeden sighed as he walked toward Gravity's stall, the horse he rode on the trails impassable by buggy. He smiled as he remembered the introduction to the horse. Jordyn had smiled and slipped into the stall. "This big guy can be yours while you're here." She rubbed his neck affectionately and Braeden laughed as the horse leaned his head against Jordyn's in a very human gesture of affection.

"Are you sure he'll let me ride him? I think he considers himself your horse."

Jordyn actually giggled at that. "He is my horse normally, but Gravity needs some experience with other riders." She looked at Braeden with solemn eyes. "But you've got to promise to be good to him. He's my miracle horse."

"I'm sure there's a story behind that description."

Jordyn stepped to the side, allowing Braeden to get acquainted with his new friend. "There is. He was being boarded in a stable not far from here and apparently someone had a grudge against the owner. He came out one morning and discovered that someone had poisoned every horse there. Our vet called in everyone with any horse sense and we worked all day and all night." Jordyn stroked the gray coat. "Gravity was my assignment and he pulled through. I talked to him all night and did everything that Doc told me to do." She smiled up at Braeden. "To be honest, I got so attached to him that night I don't know what I would have done if I had lost him. He fought so hard and kept looking at me with his big brown eyes as if to say he trusted me to fix him."

"I'm glad he made it. For both your sakes. And I promise to take good care of him."

Jordyn smiled gratefully at Braeden's sincere words. "Thanks."

Braeden couldn't help but admire her for her gentleness and kindness to everyone and everything she came in contact with. His discoveries about her true nature were only making his job more difficult. And despite his earlier hopes to get his job done as soon as possible, he wasn't any closer to getting the information he needed than he had been the night of the auction. As he groomed the spoiled Gravity, slipping him a sugar cube swiped from the bunkhouse kitchen, he decided to change that today. When she came down to the barn, he would ask her to set the date for their date. With better wording of course. Decision made, he set about cleaning Gravity's stall.

CHAPTER 6

Jordyn lay back on the couch with a groan. She had always hated being sick. Especially when it gave her mind so much time to go places she would rather it not go. All morning long, she had been trying to pull herself out of bed and out to play. However, after a short breakfast and shower that had worn her out, she knew she wasn't going out to play today. As much as she hated colds, she wasn't surprised that this one had hit her. Late nights of going through Tommy's meager possessions and any paperwork of his she could find would do that. Add the worry over the fact that she couldn't seem to find anything that would explain or assuage her suspicions and it was a wonder she hadn't been sick before now.

However, she had discovered how little she actually knew about Tommy. She had even found an old highschool yearbook of Tommy's, but his last name was Michaels, not Grey as he had introduced himself to her. She had found it amusing that their last name was the same, and when they married, convenient. But now it only raised a lot of questions about who Tommy really was and what he did before they met. As her mind bounced from one disturbing thought to another, she wondered if she had any high powered cold medicine that would shut it off.

Ensconced in her favorite pair of pajamas with tissues, her cell phone, juice, a good book, and an electric blanket, she was prepared to wait out her cold. Until tomorrow.

Forty-five minutes later, the doorbell rang and forty-five minutes two seconds later, her cell phone began yelling at her to answer the phone. Literally. The ring was obnoxious, but Mon had chosen it for her personal ringer.

"Hello," Jordyn croaked into the phone.

"Yikes! You sound terrible." Monica was always so diplomatic.

"Thanks, Mon. I'm thinking of making this my new sound. It's so low and husky, it ought to attract guys, don't you think?"

Jordyn smiled as she recognized the silhouette on the other side of the glass in the door and said into the phone, "Can you hang on a minute? There's someone at the door."

Braeden stared at Jordyn for about a millisecond before a slow smile spread across his face. If it wasn't so clichéd he'd have to say, "We need to stop meeting this way." She was in pajamas again and she clearly hadn't expected company. She had a red nose, slightly puffy eyes, and was dressed to impress in pajamas bespeckled with horses. No silk for this heiress, no designer gowns. Oversized, horsey pajamas! He almost laughed out loud at how adorably ridiculous she looked.

He removed his hat. "I'm sorry to drag you out of bed. Again. I got a little worried when you didn't show up at the barn this morning."

Monica was yelling in her ear, demanding to know who was at the door and Braeden Parker's apologetic smile was making her lose track of thought. Or was that her cold medicine?

"Come on in." She gestured toward the living room. "Have a seat and I'll bring you some coffee if you'd like." At his nod she headed toward the kitchen.

"Hello, Jordyn. I asked who was at your door?" Monica's urgent voice broke through Jordyn's distracted haze.

"What are you, my social secretary?" Jordyn couldn't help teasing Monica.

"No, I just don't think it's safe to let strangers in your house and offer them coffee." Mon's voice was less intense. But only a little.

"Well, it's not a stranger. It's Braeden Parker."

"The same Braeden Parker you paid good money to go on a date with? The one who makes your heart jump and your stomach flip? The one who you've been working..."

"Yes," Jordyn interrupted, "that Braeden Parker."

"So you admit your heart jumps over Braeden Parker." Monica's voice was annoyingly triumphant.

"No, I was merely identifying that this is the same Braeden Parker I met at the auction," Jordyn said rather too politely, "and we haven't even been on that date yet. I also would've donated the money anyway and it served a good cause to bid with it instead. I wouldn't let a stray dog I liked go on a date with Angela Beaumont."

Jordyn continued to try to refute Monica's ridiculous accusations as she made coffee. "Mon, I've really got to go."

After being ignored for the duration of the coffee being made and being treated to a mini lecture on how she should dress, act, etc., on the date she said again, "I appreciate your interest but I really, really have to go."

She almost spilled the coffee she was pouring into two mugs when the head of the subject of their conversation popped around the corner and asked, "Do you need a hand with that?"

Jordyn nodded slightly causing her cell phone to drop. Braeden ambled into the kitchen, but rather than helping with the spilled coffee he snatched the cell phone from Jordyn's unsuspecting hand, and said, "Hi, Jordyn can't come to the phone right now. Leave a message and she'll call you back." He ended the call and handed the phone back to her with what could only be called a toothy grin.

"You just can't get off of the phone with some people," he said as he inhaled the smell of coffee and…something that smelled of vanilla. He'd noticed that Jordyn always smelled like vanilla and sandalwood.

At his matter-of-fact handling of the situation, Jordyn couldn't help but chuckle a little. "I would normally agree but that happened to be one of my best friends, Monica Wallace. I'm going to have to give her a really good explanation when she calls later."

Braeden's eyebrows rose. "The Monica Wallace of Wallace Industries?"

"One and the same," Jordyn answered.

"Well, I've never insulted one of the rich and famous before."

At Jordyn's disbelieving look he qualified. "Okay, I've insulted a few donors who had no idea of the difference between conservation and preservation, but never someone I had no connection to at all."

"I'm sure she'll not hold it against you. She's probably thrilled that a man felt comfortable enough to answer my phone. If that's what you call what you did." Jordyn said it without thinking and before she realized how it would sound.

"I'm glad. I wouldn't want the best friend of my date to be mad at me."

"Your date?" Jordyn questioned, almost choking on the coffee.

"Yes. I was going to ask if you wanted that date I owe you tonight, but from the sound and look of you, I'd say that you are suffering from a spring cold and that you plan on staying in."

His glance at her pajamas made Jordyn suddenly very self-conscious..and sassy. She grinned down at her pajamas and then looked at Braeden. "You don't like my pajamas?"

"Oh, I like them. But I don't think you want your picture taken in them. It would undoubtedly hit every tabloid in the country and ruin your heiress persona." He was clearly trying not to laugh.

Jordyn sighed heavily. "I had forgotten that the highest bid date is on the brochure for next year's auction. I guess I should stay in then." She finished with a dramatic, heartfelt sigh, as if the thought of staying in her cozy home wasn't what she really wanted to do.

"Pizza."

"What?" Jordyn's brow furrowed in confusion.

"I can go get pizza and we can eat here. I'll even wait on you so you don't have to get off of the couch." He grinned. "Isn't that what every woman dreams of anyway?"

"To have a man wait on her hand and foot?" Jordyn cocked her head to the side and said, "Depends on the woman. Tonight I think I'm definitely that kind of woman."

Braeden nodded. "Then don't worry about supper. I'll be here at six sharp, pizza in tow." He put his hat on and paused at the door. "Do you need anything? I can run by the drugstore if you like?"

A glance at his eyes told her his offer was sincere. Jordyn smiled with genuine appreciation for his concern. The sincerity of his offer wasn't because she was rich and he was trying to stay on her good side. It was an offer of help from one human being to another. He wanted to help Jordyn his friend, not Jordyn Grey. The thought of him as a friend was both nice and…unsatisfying.

"I appreciate the offer, but I think I'm set. I hate taking medicine anyway so it would probably be a wasted trip."

Braeden smiled. "Me too. But please don't hesitate to call if you think of something you need. Or want."

Jordyn looked dead into his eyes and said seriously, "Thanks, Braeden."

Her appreciation made him feel happy and ashamed all at once. "Well, you jumped in and helped me when I needed it. One good turn deserves another, right? I'll see you at six."

Braeden's thoughts settled on Jordyn's farm on the drive home from The Pizza Place. Promise Land. It was a good name. According to the account, Jordyn's ancestor had led his family out of Ireland and into Tennessee with little more than a dream to keep them going. They had all settled close together and now their descendants were among the wealthiest in the nation. Braeden wondered if the old man of the clan had realized that when he had named the place. Of course, the buildings didn't resemble what he would have known, but Braeden figured Jordyn probably had a good portion of his spirit.

Braeden's phone rang and he dreaded the call that he had been waiting on.

"Parker," His voice was suddenly very professional and to the point as a result of glancing at the caller ID.

"Braeden, it's nice to finally speak with you. I was beginning to think I would have to rely on my contact in the bureau to get information on your progress."

Braeden didn't like feeling like he needed to report to at every turn. He would get the job done. Somehow.

"Have you found out anything of interest from the lovely Ms. Grey?"

Braeden rubbed a hand down his face. Yes, he had found out many things about Jordyn. She was as generous as she was wealthy, as caring as she was beautiful, and she had already suffered too much because of Tommy.

"No. I haven't found out anything definite yet." Braeden hated how cold he sounded. "And I don't have anything suspicious to report since the spliced fence." He wanted to scream at the injustice of the situation. He wanted to go to Jordyn, tell her the truth, and then just ask her for the information he needed. But if he did that, he might get her killed, as well as tell her more about Tommy than she might want to know.

"I'm having dinner with her tonight. Hopefully she'll open up and I'll have something to report tomorrow." He kept his voice brusque.

"Let's hope so. We're getting pressure from our friends at the FBI. I have been informed that they have a team there now. And we know that there are probably other eyes we don't know about." As if Braeden needed that reminder.

"Yes, I am aware of the situation."

"Take care of yourself, Braeden." Braeden recognized the gesture for what it was. An apology for putting him in this situation.

"I always do." Which was his standard reply.

The call was ended without any formal good-byes. By this time, Braeden had pulled through the gates to Promise Land and wound his way through a tree-shaded drive to sit in front of the house. The pizza suddenly didn't smell so good. He was growing increasingly concerned about the situation and his part in it.

"Lord, I need your help. I don't like the deception and I can't keep her safe on my own. She distracts me even more than my conscience does." He sighed. "I don't know how to deal with my feelings for her, Lord. Please, help me to do what's right for both of us."

He didn't feel overwhelming peace at his prayer, but he did feel the comfort of knowing that neither he nor Jordyn were alone. That thought helped put the smile on his face as he rang the doorbell.

Jordyn moved to answer the door, enjoying the soft swish of her cream-colored, floor-length skirt. For the first time in their acquaintance, she was prepared for his arrival. And she was the only one who was prepared.

Braeden was overwhelmed with feelings he didn't completely understand when Jordyn answered the door. He was used to seeing her in work clothes, but these were definitely not work clothes. Bare feet poked out from under the long skirt that fell full but fit snuggly to her hips. The soft blue sweater set off her deep red hair. She looked wonderful. But it was her welcoming smile that made him feel…happy.

"Your pizza has arrived," he said holding up the box for inspection.

"And what's this?" Jordyn asked as she snatched two items off of the pizza box.

Braeden smiled a little sheepishly as she read the titles of the two DVDs he'd brought.

"I didn't think you'd be up to playing a game." He shrugged looking like a little boy who had been caught slipping his girl a flower. Jordyn couldn't help but smile at how self-conscious he looked.

"So you brought Disney's *Robin Hood* and Cary Grant in *Charade*. That's your idea of good dating materials, huh?" She couldn't help teasing him a bit more. "A cartoon and a romantic intrigue. *Hmm*…what does that say about Braeden Parker?"

"Hey, I was just trying to pamper the sick and afflicted." Clearly his masculine pride was suffering from her gentle teasing.

She impulsively gave him a sideways hug. "Thanks. They're perfect. The cartoon for laughs and the other for the romance, intrigue, secret identities, and a few fights for you."

They decided to eat their pizza on the back patio off of the kitchen to enjoy the sunset, per Jordyn's earlier request.

Braeden gestured to a glass enclosed building adjacent to the back of the house and asked, "What's that?"

Jordyn finished chewing and swallowed before she said, "A pool." She took another bite, chewed, and swallowed before looking at Braeden.

Braeden had stopped eating. "You're serious?"

"Yes."

When Braeden continued to stare at the building she said, "Pools aren't that unusual."

"Oh I know. I was just wondering why you decided to put one in. I mean, there are no less than six beautiful ponds and a river running through your property."

Jordyn shrugged and as she looked down at her food. "It wasn't there until around two years ago." She paused slightly before saying, "It was a wedding present."

"From your dad?"

"From me." Jordyn finally met Braeden's eyes as she continued, "Tommy, my late husband, preferred the privacy and convenience of heated, enclosed, chlorinated water."

Braeden nodded and waited for her to change the subject. When she didn't he asked, "Do you use it year-round?"

Jordyn's laugh broke the tension. "I hardly use it at all, except in the winter. I let the girl scouts have their big summer bash here and Mon, Faith, and I have used it once or twice. Dave and the guys would rather go to the river if they do any swimming at all." She glanced at him and offered sincerely, "You can use it anytime you want. I usually leave the outside door open."

Braeden smiled but shook his head. "Thanks but I'd rather hit one of the ponds or the river. There's something about swimming in God's great big creation that makes me feel closer to him."

Jordyn surprised him by saying, "I always liked that better too. Pools always reminded me of country clubs and stuffy rich people. I think that's one of the reasons I always loved this place. Out on the trails, in the ponds, or wading in the river, I'm just like anybody else. Also, you can't fish in a swimming pool." She paused before she said, "I didn't know you were a Christian."

"That's sad. I should've shown that by now. I got saved when I was a teenager, even though I'd been going to church all of my life. But I can honestly say it was the best decision I ever made."

"I used to feel that way about God," Jordyn said with a sad, disillusioned smile.

"What changed your mind?" Braeden wasn't sure he wanted to open this particular topic right now. He wanted her to talk to him, but at the same time he felt guilty because he was getting paid to get close and find out her secrets. Some Christian he was being.

"Tommy's death." Jordyn's reply both surprised and bothered him. Until that moment, he hadn't acknowledged that she had genuinely loved Tommy.

Jordyn read his surprise and said, "It's not what you think. I know everyone has a time to die and that death is an essential part of life." She hesitated and asked, "Do you really want to hear this?"

"I want to get to know you and this is part of you." Braeden's answer seemed to reassure her and she continued.

"I was saved when I was six. My family have been members of the small church in town since it was established in the late 1800s. We were faithful members when we were home. On the occasions that we weren't home on Sundays, we had family prayer meeting." She paused and sighed. "So you see, I have a firm foundation for faith, even though I'm currently faithless." She glanced at him, waiting for the inevitable disapproval that some so-called Christians would heap upon her.

As if sensing how important his reaction to her admission was, Braeden shrugged one shoulder, "Faith wouldn't be faith unless it was tested." His words encouraged her to continue.

Jordyn took a deep breath before continuing her story. "I didn't make it to church much when Tommy and I started dating. As a matter of fact, I didn't make it much of anywhere after Tommy and I started dating. I'm sure missing church didn't help me. After about two months of dating, we got married and spent a relatively short two-week honeymoon on a very private island. Four weeks to the day that we came home from the honeymoon,

Tommy was killed by a hit-and-run driver. Despite my lack of attendance, our church members surrounded me with love, food, and what they deemed comfort." Bitterness edged into her voice and she twisted the napkin in her hands unmercifully. Braeden didn't think she noticed the tears that had started running down her face.

"They told me that God knew best. The more they said it, the more I questioned why." She looked up at Braeden with tortured eyes. "If God knew what was best, why did he let Tommy die?"

Braeden wanted to stop the rapid flow of words. He wanted to kiss away the tears that had found their way down her soft cheeks and tell her that the pain really would go away. Instead, he just listened.

"You see, I'd prayed about marrying Tommy before I married him. I've been taught about God's will and I knew that I wanted only his will in my life. Tommy made me so happy I just knew he was the one God had for me. I prayed that he would change my feelings for Tommy if it wasn't his will. Instead, they grew stronger. Everyone in my life had reservations about Tommy and our relationship, but I had prayed and in that I felt secure. I had prayed for God's will and I felt that Tommy was his will for me."

Braeden was a bit confused and it showed when he said, "Just because Tommy died so early in life doesn't mean that your marriage wasn't the Lord's will. I'm not saying that I think you were or were not in his will, but Tommy's death shouldn't be the only measure."

Jordyn's laugh grated. "His premature death isn't what makes me angry and doubtful. We had a blissful courtship and a wonderful honeymoon." Jordyn's hands were clenched onto her chair arms so tightly he wasn't sure they would come loose. The napkin lay in a tattered mess in her lap.

"As soon as we got home, we started fighting. And we fought over the stupidest things. He'd promised to go to church with me, saying he wanted to be part of everything in my life. When we got home, he wouldn't even let me go. In fact, he wouldn't let me go anywhere without him. He would get calls on his cell phone and leave the room to talk. I began to wonder if he was having an affair and when I asked him about it he said he wasn't going to tell me about the phone calls for my own good and that he didn't want me to ask him about them again. I thought we'd had this beautiful, special relationship. I value honesty and trust more than most, and I thought we had the kind of relationship where we were honest and truthful about everything."

The anguish in her voice shocked Braeden and her story made him wonder if she knew anything at all about Tommy's past.

"Our relationship was of the kind you always dream about. I felt so blessed and…content. Then everything changed. When our elopement was made public with the details of Dad giving Promise Land to us as a wedding present, he was furious. We argued. And then when I wanted to go to town the next day and he wouldn't let me, we argued again…and again. I blamed him for being irrational and jealous. He blamed me for being stubborn and spoiled. It was our worst fight yet and we both said a lot of things we didn't mean." Her voice grew soft and desperately hopeful. "At least, I hope we didn't mean them. I finally accused him of acting as if he regretted marrying me. He said he did and then left."

The pain and guilt in Jordyn's eyes made Braeden reach for her hand.

"I never saw him alive again." Jordyn's voice had fallen to little more than a whisper. She fell silent for a moment before finally looking directly at Braeden, whose face was partially concealed by the falling darkness. "I don't blame God for Tommy's death. I blame him for letting me love Tommy, when obviously I shouldn't have. I blame him for letting me marry Tommy and making his last days on this earth miserable. I blame him for not changing how I felt about Tommy when I prayed that he would. I blame him for the guilt of knowing that if I hadn't married Tommy, he'd be alive."

Braeden couldn't stay in his chair. He knelt in front of Jordyn and wiped the tears that were falling rapidly but silently. He wanted to explain that Tommy had loved her, that his actions were because he loved her. He wanted to tell her that Tommy regretted marrying her for the danger and stress it was putting on her, not because he didn't want her. But he couldn't. "Jordyn, you didn't cause Tommy's death."

"Oh Lord"—he prayed silently—"give me the words to soothe her tortured soul and point her back to you. Give me the words she needs to hear."

"Maybe Tommy wouldn't have lived as long as he did if you hadn't married him. Maybe he realized how much he loved you and that's why he was so protective. He might have been afraid of losing you and just took protecting you way too far." Braeden's voice grew more urgent as he said, "Jordyn, maybe you fulfilled the Lord's will in marrying Tommy and keeping him alive long enough to hear about God."

"If that's true then it was God's will that Tommy die!" She was both angry and confused. "How could that be the will of a loving Father? To let me love Tommy with the intent of taking him away?"

Braeden swallowed hard, both hands resting on Jordyn's shoulders. "Remember Job. It wasn't God's will that Job lose everything and suffer as he did, but God allowed it to happen. Sometimes evil does affect good people. What we as Christians have to do is love God and let him turn our circumstances to our good. In the end, it will serve God's purpose."

"But what possible purpose could Tommy's death serve?" Jordyn's voice was ragged with emotions that had been pent up far too long.

"Only he knows. We find out when and if he shows us." Braeden shrugged as he said, "That's why we call it faith."

Jordyn shook her head doubtfully. "How can a mere human being have enough faith?"

"We don't. All we need is faith as large as a grain of mustard seed. God will take care of the rest. He'll never push us past what we can endure and he's always right there to carry us when our meager human faith fails. He'll always be there to help, all we have to do is let him."

They sat in the darkness for a while. Braeden holding both of her hands as she cried out a lot of pain and heartache. When she had been quiet for several minutes, Braeden plucked a napkin off of the table and wiped her eyes, her face, and her nose.

"I think you've sat around too much today. And I'm sure you missed crawling through briars and brush to download pictures and check habitat. How about that movie?"

Jordyn gave him a small, slightly embarrassed smile as they moved into the kitchen with the remnants of their meal.

"Sounds good, but it needs to be the cartoon. I don't think I could take *Charade* tonight."

As they moved to the living room, Braeden couldn't help but feel relieved. He didn't think he could watch that movie either and not tell her everything. It was all he could do not to tell her that he knew Tommy wasn't having an affair. He'd been trying to protect her from his past. The problem with the past was that it eventually caught up with your present.

Well, he was reasonably certain she didn't know anything that was significant. Their conversation had put his earlier suspicions to rest. In a way, he was glad she didn't. It would make her safer. But her lack of knowledge was key in causing her heartbreak. He didn't pause to wonder at the fact that her innocence in the whole situation was going to make his job harder. He was putting the feelings of the subject ahead of the job. That could make the situation much more dangerous than he had anticipated. For both of them.

The next day, Jordyn sat in the kitchen, debating whether or not to venture outside. She had still felt lousy that morning, but was feeling considerably better this afternoon. Just as she decided to head outside, her cell phone rang. Scooping it off of the kitchen counter, Jordyn frowned at the caller ID.

"Unavailable. Well, if you're unavailable, so am I."

She ignored the call and headed to the door.

Braeden watched as Jordyn made her way to the barn. He couldn't help but smile as he remembered her surprise when he'd informed her that last night's pizza was not there official date.

"Oh really. So when do you intend to fulfill your obligations, Mr. Parker?"

She had asked it so teasingly that he'd responded in kind.

"When you least expect it, Ms. Grey. And if you knew me better, you would know that pizza on the back porch isn't a date. That's an evening with a friend."

Jordyn had smiled and said, "Well friend, I'm having spaghetti tonight if you care to join me."

Braeden cocked his head as if in great consideration, a frown of concentration on his face.

"I don't know. Is it homemade or out of a jar?"

Jordyn answered with equal mock seriousness. "It's homemade."

He rubbed his chin in a gesture of deep thought. "With bread?"

"Yes."

"And something chocolate for desert?"

"Yes."

A smile replaced the frown and he nodded decidedly. "I'll be there. What time is dinner?"

Jordyn shrugged. "Six-thirty okay with you?"

Braeden nodded. "Anytime is fine with me when somebody's feeding me. What should I bring?"

"Something unusual to drink."

Braeden blinked. He'd expected the usual waved hand telling him not to bother. Instead, she had made an interesting request.

He smiled. "Deal. See ya at six-thirty tomorrow."

Even though it wasn't dinner time yet, Braeden was glad to see Jordyn making her way to the barns. Too glad in fact.

"How's the cold?" He called to her.

Jordyn scrunched her nose. "Making its presence less felt but not gone."

"If you like I can go get dinner again."

"Nah, that'd take all of the productive activity out of my day if you did that"—she said smilingly—"besides I'm looking forward to what you bring to drink."

"Did you come all the way out here, cold and all, just to try and wheedle what I'm bringing out of me?" He shook his head and clucked disapprovingly. "I'm surprised at you, Ms. Grey. I expected more from a well-brought up young lady."

His truly pathetic Southern accent and equally wounded expression brought a peal of laughter from Jordyn.

"Okay, if you won't tell me, I'll just find out tonight." She moved toward the barn where a favorite mare was currently residing and called over her shoulder. "But you just wait. One of these days you'll need to know something and I'm not going to tell you."

If she had turned around, she would have seen his smile die and his face grow ever so slightly pale. She couldn't have jolted him more if she had claimed to be a long lost princess.

"I hope you don't do that, Jordyn," he said softly to her retreating form. "I really hope you don't do that."

CHAPTER 7

"So, how's it going with Braeden?" The question was directed at Jordyn who was staring down at her drink, absently twirling her straw in her whipped cream. When she didn't respond, Faith said, "I think we should all dye our hair purple, don't you Jordyn?"

Both Faith and Monica had trouble containing their laughter when Jordyn gave a distracted, "Umhm."

"And," Monica added, "then we should wear body suits and run up and down Main Street yelling at passing drivers! Our personal spin on Lady Godiva. What do you think?"

"That sounds good," Jordyn answered as she finally looked up at her two grinning friends. Her puzzled look at their amusement sent them over the edge. Their hoots of laughter made Jordyn smile and shrug. Her obvious confusion made them laugh all the harder. Jordyn began to turn slightly pink as she noticed other diners looking their way.

"What's so funny?" her question set off another burst of laughter. Jordyn decided to sit and smile until her apparently uncontrollable friends stopped laughing. She sat back and crossed her arms.

When they didn't stop and tears of hilarity began to trickle down their faces, she too joined in the laughter.

"Okay," she said a little breathlessly. "What's so funny?"

Jordyn's question brought additional laughter just as they were getting control.

Faith took pity on her. "You, you agreed to—" She had to stop for fear of losing control all over again.

Monica wiped her eyes and took a sip of her ginger ale, trying to compose herself.

Jordyn kept looking from one to the other. Finally, Monica told her what was so funny.

"We asked you a question and when you didn't hear us, Faith decided we should all dye our hair purple. You agreed with her so I decided we should don body suits and run up and down the street yelling at drivers." Monica was smiling from ear to ear. "You thought that was a good idea too." It was clearly evident that Monica's laughter was near to bubbling over again.

Jordyn had to chuckle at herself. "I guess my mind was wondering." She offered in sheepish explanation.

"We noticed that," Faith dryly interjected, "what we want to know is where your mind was wondering to?"

"Oh we don't need her to tell us that, Faith," Monica spoke and gave a mischievous wink. "I'd say it was back at Promise Land where a certain handsome wildlife biologist is right now."

Jordyn shook her head. "Well, you're wrong. He was gone when I left this morning and I haven't seen or heard from him all day."

Jordyn didn't realize how much her comments showed the depths of her growing feelings. Monica and Faith surreptitiously glanced at one another and then they both stared at Jordyn. Faith surprised them all by asking, "Why do you care?"

"What?" Jordyn's question came out in a surprised whoosh.

"Why...do you...care?" Faith repeated.

Jordyn stared at her and then out the window while trying to figure out the answer. She cared about Braeden as a person. She cared about him as a friend. She definitely cared about his work.

She was about to answer with her thoughts when a nagging voice reminded her that she didn't get this uptight when Mon or Faith didn't call her. So, why did she care so much about Braeden?

"I honestly don't know," the genuine confusion in Jordyn's eyes and the frustration in her voice kept them from telling her outright that she was investing her heart in Braeden.

"Yes, you do," Monica insisted. "Think real hard." Her voice was both demanding and coaxing.

"I honestly don't know." Jordyn's normally imperturbable voice was sounding a bit testy.

Faith smiled at her with a knowing smile. "Honey, you are finally romantically interested in the man."

"No, I'm not." Jordyn instantly denied.

"Yes, you are." Monica agreed with Faith.

"No, I'm really not. It's something else."

"Yes, you are." Monica and Faith chorused.

"And you don't want to admit it because it scares the living daylights out of you," Monica added.

Jordyn stared at them. *Could they be right?* She knew she was attracted to Braeden, but attraction didn't mean she wanted a romantic relationship with him. She enjoyed being with him and she valued his friendship, but that was a far cry from dating. Wasn't it? Since the evening of the pizza delivery, they had shared dinner together almost every night. Unless he had more work to do after they got back from checking cameras and habitat. She started as she realized that the pizza dinner had been weeks ago and that they had spent a lot of time together since then, both working and socially.

She had frequently thought about what he'd said about Tommy and God's will. She had even started reading her Bible again and she was planning to go to church this Sunday. The Scriptures she needed always seemed to be the ones she read. For the first time in a long time she was feeling... peaceful. Despite all of this, she was sure she wasn't ready for a relationship with

Braeden. Even if she was, Braeden didn't appear interested in a relationship with her. She had thought he might be, but every time he had an opportunity to take the first step, he held back.

Monica watched Jordyn's face as her thoughts flew. As usual, she read Jordyn correctly. "Don't analyze it, Jordyn. If there's something between you and Braeden, just enjoy it."

Hours later, when night had fallen and there was still no Braeden, Jordyn was scoffing at the advice. "I'd enjoy a root canal as much as I'd enjoy the pressure of a relationship right now." She would probably have been grateful that he was gone if she had been privy to Monica's conversation at that very moment.

Monica was staring at the tall man she now knew as Luke Stettleman with ill-concealed rage.

"They what?" Her low voiced question might as well have been shouted for all of the venom injected in it.

"I repeat. The US Marshal's Service felt we may need some help with the situation and sent in an undercover agent of sorts." His irritation at having to repeat himself only added fuel to Monica's angry fire.

"An undercover agent to do what? Spy on every move Jordyn makes? Besides, isn't doing that illegal or something?"

"No, I believe he is supposed to ascertain what, if anything, she knows. He wants to find out what Tommy did with the papers. And it's not illegal. It's a joint operation so they can do what they want and be within their jurisdiction." Monica had to stop a smile as he added softly, "Even if it is downright rude and insulting."

"Like Jordyn is going to tell a complete stranger personal details about her life?"

"Well, you're her friend and she's apparently not talking to you. I guess they decided to try a different tactic." His tone clearly implied what he thought of her investigative skills.

"Do we know who it is?" Monica's voice was resigned.

She didn't miss the twinge of irritation when he said, "Apparently, that's a need-to-know basis."

Monica's eyebrows rose. "You mean you don't know?"

"I mean I don't know and I am not likely to be told." His voice clearly implied that he didn't like being left in the dark, while his blue eyes shot sparks at her for pointing out the fact that he wasn't considered an essential part of the operation by everyone involved. "I don't particularly like working with the high and mighty US Marshal's Service.

"Well, I think we're finally in agreement over something."

He arrogantly arched one blonde brow. "Break out the record books."

"Your sarcasm is not appreciated." Monica said as she bent slightly over the golf ball. She was getting very weary of dealing with this Luke character. It would help if she were equally tired of looking at him.

She almost smiled at how ludicrous their conversation was. They had planned the covert meeting for a miniature golf course in downtown Pigeon Forge. He'd shown up wearing jeans, tennis shoes, and a blue T-shirt that matched his eyes.

They were talking as they moved from one hole to another. While Monica had been wool gathering, another couple had moved toward them. She just about dropped her putter when Luke said, "No honey, you're doing it all wrong."

He moved up behind her, put his arms around her, and corrected her swing.

"Is this really necessary?" Monica hissed.

"Do you think I'd be doing it if it weren't necessary." He whispered in her ear. "We can't have people thinking you're at a covert meeting with the FBI."

His calmness infuriated her. She didn't know if it was because her heart was flying or if it was just because he had the power to irritate her.

She stared as the ball they'd hit went directly into the hole.

"Thanks, sweetie," Monica said loudly. Then she tilted her head and kissed him on the lips. She broke his hold on her and shashayed her way to the next hole, out of earshot of the couple.

"So, are you going to get the information for me?" Monica's voice was surprisingly normal.

"What?" Luke asked.

It was nice to know she could befuddle him. At Monica's raised brow he said, "And how do you propose I do that?"

Monica shrugged. "Tell the high and mighty US Marshal's Service that I'm inept, jumpy, and that I'm liable to accidentally shoot their guy if I don't know who he is."

"Hey, that's not a bad idea."

Monica was tempted to swing the putter at his head instead of at her little red ball. He must have realized it too because he took a step back and looked perfectly prepared to defend himself.

"If you're so close to Jordyn, wouldn't you know if there was someone new in her life? Has she hired a new cleaning service, a new farm hand, or something?"

He asked the question just as Monica swung. He laughed as her ball went over the side of the fake barnyard and into the fake creek.

"Hey, that was your best…" His voice trailed off as he looked back at Monica. She had frozen in place. Her face had gone pale, and the anger in her eyes stopped him from making a move toward her. He was alarmed to also see a very deep concern.

"I can't believe they would go that far to get those papers," she had whispered but he heard her.

"What exactly did they do?" Luke questioned.

"Luke, do you know who is in contact with the undercover agent?"

"Yes, I have a meeting with him tomorrow to swap some information." Luke's voice was all business, his eyes watching carefully as Monica retrieved her ball and set up for another shot.

"Don't go." She swung and the ball rolled neatly into the hole.

"You want me to cancel an information exchange meeting with the U.S. Marshal's Service?" Luke's voice was disbelieving.

Monica met his gaze calmly as he set up his shot. "No, I don't want you to cancel it." Just as he was starting to feel relieved she added, "I want you to be a no-show."

He missed the shot. "I can't do that. I need to know who their inside man is and I can't find that out if I make them mad by not showing up." He explained it in a tone that implied she was too dumb to understand the situation.

"Aren't we the ones handing over most of the information?"

"Yes."

"Then I wouldn't worry about it." Monica swung her putter onto her shoulder in a pose that made her look completely at ease and in control. Luke was glad that someone felt that way. "I'll let you know if their guy finds out anything."

Luke smiled as he stepped out of her way. Maybe she wasn't such a bad agent. "You know who he is."

"Yes," she said as she sent the ball sailing into the hole. When she looked up she found Luke smiling at her as if she were his ace in the hole.

"I almost pity the man. Are you going to tell me who it is?"

Monica gave him a small, sad smile. "Unfortunately, it's Jordyn's new boyfriend."

CHAPTER 8

Jordyn sat in the Grey family pew feeling more than a little awkward. Folks noticed her unusual presence, but only smiled and nodded greetings.

Ann, a seventy year-old wonder, sat in the pew in front of Jordyn. As a pastor's wife for over thirty years, she just seemed to know what folks needed even before they did. When her eyes landed on Jordyn, her round face lit with a smile.

Jordyn heard her name called and turned with a smile of her own for Ann. She couldn't have stopped the smile if she had wanted to, which she didn't. She went willingly into the arms of the petite woman, feeling more welcome than ever.

"Oh child, it's so good to see you sitting where you belong," Ann's words made Jordyn's eyes sting.

"I know it's been a long, painful road back, Jordyn. But the first step to healing is recognizing your need to be healed." Ann's words were exactly what Jordyn needed to hear. She hugged the older woman tight before slipping back into her pew just as Pastor Charles, the pastor of the country church for thirty years, stepped up to the pulpit.

At this point in their ministry, he and Ann had known most of the people in their church from the day they were born. Now, they were watching as the babies they helped dedicate were bringing babies of their own to church. They were the best people to walk the earth in Jordyn's mind. They had lived their teachings. Even as a rebellious teenager, Jordyn had always thought them the most Christ-like people in the world. She knew without being told that while she was absent from the church, they had prayed for her every day, never giving up hope that she would come back. She cringed with the knowledge that she had been a burden to the couple.

Pastor Charles smiled as he greeted the congregation. "It's wonderful to see all you beautiful people here with us this Lord's day. Your faces tell me that the Lord is truly good."

His eyes landed on Jordyn and his face, already creased with a smile, lit up. "And it's also an answer to prayer to have someone sitting in the Grey pew this morning."

Jordyn returned his smile and felt herself blush at the chorus of "amens" echoing in the congregation. Ann reached back and gently squeezed Jordyn's hand. Despite her embarrassment at the public acknowledgement, Jordyn couldn't help but feel that she was home.

After the congregational singing, Jordyn listened as the youth group sang a song their previous youth pastor had written before he succumbed to cancer. She felt tears fall as they sang about trusting the Lord and following him despite any circumstance.

Jordyn stood with the rest of the congregation during the song with her head bowed. As the sweet young voices sang of their faith, Jordyn turned the words into a personal prayer. She asked for God's forgiveness for her doubt and her bitterness. She asked for his help and strength. She prayed for his will in her life, trusting that he would work for her. Before the song was over, her heart felt near to bursting over God's goodness and his forgiveness. It amazed her that despite how undeserving she was, he had always been there waiting for her to reach for him.

Ann slipped into her pew, pressing tissues into Jordyn's hand and slipping her arm around Jordyn's waist. Without having to explain, Jordyn knew that Ann understood that her tears were no longer tears of pain and grief, but of joy.

Ann settled in beside Jordyn for the message after the song ended and the tearful group had found their seats. Pastor Charles prepared for hours to give his congregation what the Lord had laid on his heart. Today was no different. Jordyn found herself smiling as Pastor Charles spoke about God's name.

"It is often said that the Christian God has no name and this makes him less accessible. I heard this as a young man and I hear it's still mentioned today. The fact is, the Christian God has more names than any other. He is *the* God. No other god of this world is referred to with a capital *G*. He is the Prince of Peace. He is the Comforter. He is many things and he is everything we need."

"Today I would like to talk about the names of God that are tended to be overlooked in the alphabet of God's names. Jehovah-jireh, the Lord will provide. Jehovah-nissi, the Lord my banner. Jehovah-shalom, the Lord send peace. Jehovah-shammah, the Lord is there. Jehovah-tsidkenu, the Lord our Righteousness."

Jordyn reflected on the reasons for each name and listened as Pastor Charles spoke, his age-roughened voice expounding on the greatness of God.

"Jehovah-jireh appears in Genesis 22:14. We are all familiar with the story of Abraham and Isaac and how the Lord provided the ram in lieu of Isaac as a sacrifice. However, I have found that in reading the story I have overlooked what Abraham called the altar where he offered the ram to God. He called it Jehovah-jireh, which translates the Lord will provide.

"In considering Abraham's situation, it is clear to us how the Lord provided for Abraham. He provided him with a son in his later years. When Abraham showed an obedient heart with his willingness to sacrifice Isaac, the Lord provided the sacrifice. In

Abraham's last second of desperation, before he plunged the knife into Isaac, the Lord did provide.

"The Lord is the same yesterday, today, and forever. The same God that provided for Abraham can provide for you. No matter what it is that you are facing, the Lord will provide what you need. If you need a job, a home, a car. If you need strength, if you need help, the Lord will provide. He is Jehovah-jireh. Your Provider.

Jehovah-nissi is found in Exodus 17:15. The Israelites are at war and they have received God's promise to "put out the memory of Amalek". Upon receiving this promise, Moses builds an altar. He calls this altar Jehovah-nissi which means the Lord my banner. When we are in battle, we follow the flag—the banner of our country. When we are in a situation we don't feel we can handle, when we feel we can't fight the battle, all we have to do is look for Jehovah-nissi. The Lord is our banner. Your battle is not lost as long as you follow Jehovah-nissi.

"In Judges 6:24, we read of Jehovah-shalom. We know the story of Gideon. We know how the angel of the Lord appeared unto Gideon in preparation for Gideon to lead the Israelites in conquering the Midianites. When Gideon recognized that he had spoken to an angel of the Lord, he built an altar."

Several heads nodded as the congregation drank up the words. Everyone except two year-old Johnny Cole, who had managed to escape his mother by crawling from the back to the front under the pews. But instead of running around in triumph, once he made it to the front, he pulled his diapered bottom onto the altar and sat looking up at Pastor Charles, who was smiling down at him. Pastor Charles waved away the boy's anxious and embarrassed mother and said, "He seems to have found where he felt he should be."

As Johnny's mom settled back into her seat, Pastor Charles continued.

"Gideon called the altar Jehovah-shalom, the Lord sends peace. Gideon hadn't yet beaten the Midianites, so peace was not with Israel yet. He knew that if he followed the Lord into battle that the Lord would provide all they needed to obtain victory. When you are following Jehovah-nissi and holding to the promise of Jehovah-jireh, remember Jehovah-shalom. The Lord will send you peace. Sometimes the Lord doesn't see fit to tell the storm, "Peace, be still" but instead provides you peace in the storm."

Jehovah-shammah means the Lord is there. The story for this name is found in Ezekiel 48:35. It appears in the last verse of the book of Ezekiel and says "the name of the city from that day shall be, the Lord is there." The chapter is speaking of the portions of the twelve tribes. It is a prophecy. In speaking of the major city of Israel, the Bible says the Lord is there. Now, we've seen how the father of the Israelites, Abraham, says the Lord will provide. We saw how Moses followed God's banner, and how Gideon found peace through God for his people. This prophecy of Ezekiel is referring to the millennial reign of Christ. After all the Israelites have went through, in the end the Lord is there in their city. This is also a promise to us. He promised he would never leave us nor forsake us. When you need him, he is there.

"Last but not least, we have Jehovah-tsidkenu," Pastor Charles smiled.

"Pronouncing it correctly isn't as important as understanding it thankfully. It means the Lord our righteousness and the Scripture reference is found in Jeremiah 23:6 and 33:16. Jeremiah 23:6 tells us that Jesus is Jehovah-tsidkenu, the Lord our Righteousness. In 33:16, Jerusalem is called the Lord our Righteousness when Jesus is there. This tells me that the battle we followed the Lord through, the battle for which he provided every need, the battle he gave us peace about, the battle we fought with the Lord there by our side ends with Jesus at the other end, inhabiting the city of our heart."

"When you're going through a battle, remember Jehovah-nissi. When you feel like help isn't coming from any direction, remember Jehovah-jireh. Remember that before you can build a city where Jesus dwells, you have to build an altar. No matter what, the Lord in all his righteous glory will be with you. He is Emmanuel. When you think about it and try to grasp the enormity of who God is and what he does for each of us, your heart will be overwhelmed long before your finite mind comprehends the full goodness of an infinite God. Your praises will even be a reminder of his presence because he even inhabits the praises of his people. So, when you walk in this world, give a thought to Jehovah and praise him for all of his names."

That evening found Jordyn sitting on her swing, slowly swaying in the breeze. She hadn't felt so at peace in a long time. She felt humbled and truly grateful that the almighty God cared so much for her. She had to admit, the sermon seemed different when she saw it through her new eyes. Yes, she was still worried and confused over the searched vehicle, the spliced fence, and Tommy's name, but she felt at peace. She was still basking in her wonder at God's goodness when Braeden's truck came into view.

For the first time she felt no apprehension at her developing feelings. She knew the Lord would take care of her. And she was willing to trust him to do so. She smiled as he parked his truck next to the barn and headed toward the porch. She returned his greeting smile as he settled into a sitting position, with his back leaning against one of the many porch columns.

"Did you have a good trip?" He had left Friday morning to check on his house and mail, and to touch base with the university.

He nodded. "Yes, it was good. But I must admit I was looking forward to getting back. It's so peaceful here."

At her silence, he looked at her instead of the beautiful countryside. "Even you look peaceful."

Her smile spread slowly as she kept her gaze on the falling sun, unaware of the picture she made sitting in its golden rays. "I am. The Lord and I had a nice long talk. I think I'm finally back on track."

"That's good," Braeden said softly.

"I think so too." Jordyn was quiet after that. They sat for almost an hour, exchanging an occasional comment, but mostly sitting in silence as they watched the sun dip below the horizon and listening as the evening songs broke out.

Chapter 9

The next day found the two of them in a buggy headed out to set leghold traps. When he first started talking about trapping, Jordyn's eyes had rounded in horror.

"I know what you're thinking," Braeden said on a laugh, "but these are not the metal claw traps you see in the movies. They are basically a piece of rubberized wire that tightens around the ankle when the pan, or trigger, is stepped on. The rubber keeps the skin from being cut and attached springs and swivels ensure that no bones are broken. They're just fine when we let them go."

Jordyn had nodded in understanding but still had a slightly dubious expression. Despite her obvious doubt she helped him prepare the traps for being set after a demonstration of how they wouldn't even break a stick. First, they boiled the traps in a special cleaning solution to remove all trace of human scent. Then they packed them in a clean bucket, carefully handling them with latex gloves to keep the transference of human scent at a minimum.

After loading the buggy, they drove to the path leading to the first trap site and headed up the dim trail. Braden carried the trap and "bait." Jordyn carried a bucket holding a kitchen sifter, a small bucket, a hammer, and several stakes.

Braeden walked to an area where two game paths diverged and where they had gotten several pictures of the wolves. The path that branched into two paths at this particular spot lead to a popular fence crossing. He smiled. "This ought to be the ticket. This divergent path is where they would mark their territory. Maybe I can get them to stop here long enough to say hi."

He walked toward a spot about three feet from a laurel bush and about five feet off of the trail. "Can I have the shovel please?"

Jordyn handed him the shovel and asked, "Why so close to the bush?"

"Because if I were a wolf, I would like a nice place like this to mark my territory." He looked up at Jordyn with a wide grin. "Wolves don't do the tire thing. Besides, all of the GPS data on the tagged wolves indicate they use this trail a lot."

"Oh," Jordyn replied as she watched him dig a shallow indentation in the ground. He very carefully placed the trap in the indention he'd made and then handed Jordyn the shovel.

"Will you bring me a shovel full of the driest dirt you can find?"

As Jordyn headed off for the dirt, Braeden set the trap and tripped it once to again make sure it was working properly. By the time he had attached the chain of the trap to one of the stakes and pounded the stake into the ground, Jordyn was back with a bucket full of dry dirt.

"I figured dry dirt is going to be hard to come by so I filled the bucket."

Braeden nodded, intent on his task. "Good thinking. You can't sift damp dirt so easily."

He finished adjusting everything and took the bucket of dirt, pouring some into the kitchen sifter. He shook it and dirt began covering all signs of the trap, the chain, and the stake.

"All done." He announced and placed all of the tools in a bucket.

As Jordyn started down the trail again, she glanced back to spy Braeden at the laurel bush spraying some awful smelling concoction on it, which Jordyn got the full benefit of since she was downwind.

"What in the world is that stuff?" Jordyn scrunched her nose as the smell wafted toward her.

As they headed down the trail together, Braeden grinned at her reaction, "It smells terrible, doesn't it?"

"Yes, and you could sound a little less happy about it." Jordyn teased.

Braeden laughed a little and shook his head. "I'm very happy about the smell. I've worked for a very long time to come up with a scent that wolves respond to. I think it's a very nice scent."

As Jordyn climbed into the buggy she asked, "So if you ever say I smell nice, I should immediately seek out the nearest shower?"

"Oh, no! What smells nice to humans really stinks to a wolf, except for food maybe. My smelly concoction is their version of cologne or perfume." He glanced at Jordyn. "You would stink to them even after a shower. To me, you smell very nice."

Jordyn looked doubtful. "I'm still not sure if I've been insulted or complimented."

"It's definitely a compliment. After working with stuff like that,"—he jerked his head in the direction they'd come from—"I know what smells good and you my dear, definitely smell good. Like vanilla."

"Well, coming from such an obviously trained nose, I thank you for the compliment."

They rode in silence for a minute before Jordyn asked, "How many traps are we going to set?"

Braeden shrugged. "I did most of the habitat evaluation already. All I'm doing now is checking the cams. I figure a dozen traps will be all I can handle though, especially if I catch more than two wolves in one day."

Jordyn wondered at the chances of catching even one of the elusive animals. "How often do you have to check them?"

"The law says at least once every twenty-four hours. I'll probably check them every morning and every evening."

After setting yet another trap Jordyn said, "So, the most odiferous scent I've ever smelled is your special way of asking nicely for the wolves to come."

"See, I told you that the secret was worth waiting for," Braeden said on a laugh.

"I could have waited longer before I had to smell that stuff," Jordyn said with her nose scrunched up and a green look on her face. Braeden's hoot of laughter echoed across the field.

They spent the rest of the day and much of the evening setting traps. They ate pizza that night, both too tired to tackle anything bigger than a phone call. After they'd cleaned up and eaten, they sat in Jordyn's living room watching a Discovery Channel episode on sharks. Braeden was surprised at Jordyn's knowledge until she told him that she had considered being a marine biologist.

"I also wanted to be a princess and a barrel racer as well though," she said with an impish grin.

Braeden cocked an eyebrow. "You wanted to be a barrel racing princess? I'm curious as to how you planned to manage that."

Jordyn shoved his arm playfully. "Not both at the same time. I wanted to be a princess when I was in kindergarten. I wanted to be a barrel racer when I was in elementary school."

Braeden laughed at that. He could easily picture her as either.

At nine-thirty that evening, Braeden looked down at Jordyn. About an hour ago, she had ended up stuffing a pillow in his lap with her head landing there not two seconds afterward. She was now fast asleep. Braeden smoothed her hair off of her forehead, enjoying the intimacy of the touch. It was at that moment that he realized how much he cared for Jordyn Grey. She was smart, kind, courageous, funny, and beautiful to boot. He'd noticed a change in her since he got back from the university. Her talk with the Lord as she had put it had made her seem softer somehow.

He loved being with her. He loved seeing the world through her eyes. And to him she was completely unattainable.

He gently scooted out from under her head barely causing her to stir. He was in love with her. He hadn't seen that coming. He'd been prepared to not even like her and now he was in love with the most unreachable woman he could have fallen for, short of an actual princess.

He made his way to his apartment, thinking about the predicament he'd gotten himself in. Hours later, he was still praying for answers.

CHAPTER 10

Jordyn had risen early in anticipation of her day and her call from Patrick and Dinah Grey. Braeden said he was going to check a few of the more inaccessible traps and then swing back by for her later in the morning because she had to wait on a phone call from her parents who were in Scotland for a wedding.

Jordyn dreaded the thought, but decided to, once again, search for anything in the files that might give her some clue as to what was going on. The answer had to be there staring her in the face. What did Tommy's fatal hit-and-run, a spliced fence, and a searched car have in common? Files were piled on the desk and she was getting a headache from staring at old phone records when her phone rang.

"Hello," she answered.

"Hey, sweetheart." Her father's voice sounded like he was next door instead of thousands of miles away.

"Hi, Dad," Jordyn said joyfully. "How's Scotland?"

His laughter made Jordyn smile. She could easily see his face, creased from a million smiles. "It's great. We haven't been here in years and your mother is making me go to all of the places we went to on our first trip. Tomorrow we're going back to the bed and breakfast we stayed at ten years ago. It's still open and ran by the same family." His voice faded and she heard muffled sounds and then, "Your mom wants to talk to you."

Jordyn laughed inwardly. That's how it had always been. Her dad would call and talk for about thirty seconds and then pass her off to her mother. She was glad they were having such a good time.

"Hey, how's life on the farm?" Dinah's voice held excitement and joy at talking to her only daughter.

"It's fine. We're in the middle of the wolf study I told you about a couple of weeks ago. But you know all about the farm, how's Scotland treating you?"

"Oh Jordyn, it's beautiful! I had forgotten how much it reminded me of home. With the exception of the trees. They don't have as many as we do, but it's still absolutely gorgeous. I think we're going to spend a few days in Edinburgh before we fly home. Why don't you come and join us?"

Jordyn would have loved to see Scotland again. She had gone on a trip through the United Kingdom when she was in college and she had fallen in love with Scotland. The history, its people, and its culture we're especially fascinating to her. Ireland would always be the home of her ancestors, but that didn't mean she couldn't love Scotland. In fact, there was a family story about a certain young Irish girl who was sent to live with relatives in London after her family died. After the family's refusal to let her marry her true love, she had ran off to Gretna Green. Jordyn smiled as she pictured the pipers and remembered the atmosphere at Gretna Green. "I would like to Mom, but I'm helping Dr. Parker with the wolf study. The graduate students that had planned to help him couldn't adjust to the change in schedule after he decided to do it earlier. I can't leave him to do it all himself."

There was silence on the other end for a moment. Jordyn held her breath. Her mother knew her very well, and she had a feeling that her voice had betrayed more about her relationship with Dr.

Braeden Parker than she had wanted. Her mother's next words confirmed her suspicion.

"So, tell me about this Dr. Parker, dear."

Jordyn took a deep breath. "He has a Ph.D. in Wildlife Biology and he's teaching at Dad's favorite university in Virginia. He—"

"That's not what I meant, Jordyn." Her mother's voice cut in. "What do you think of the good doctor?"

Jordyn stared out at the fields visible beyond the big study windows. What did she think of Braeden? "I think he's intelligent and ambitious. I don't think I've met someone who likes their job any more than he does. He's caring and fun to be around. He's very good-looking, but in a rugged way. I can see him as a lumberjack easier than teaching a class. When he talks to you, he gives you his full attention. He has a nice smile and…"

Jordyn trailed off as she remembered the pizza and how often he checked to make sure she was making it on the rough trails. "He's caring." She paused thinking back to how her parents had reacted to Tommy. "I think you'd like him."

"I'm sure we would, based on your description." Dinah asked gently, "How're you doing?"

"I'm fine. I think I'm finally moving on, Ma." Jordyn felt tears prick her eyes. "I had a long talk with the Lord about it and he has already helped me tremendously."

"You don't know how pleased I am to hear that. We have been praying for that specifically for a long time."

"I know," Jordyn was hard pressed to hold back the tears. She did know how much her parents cared and how they had prayed for her.

"Jordyn, I have so much more to say, but I have to go. We will be down to see you as soon as we can. I love you, Jordyn."

"I love you guys."

The soft click ended the physical connection, but Jordyn still felt close to her parents. She was so grateful for good Godly parents. She would even have been more grateful if she could have heard the conversation they were having.

Patrick stared intently at his wife as she wiped a tear off of her cheek. "She's in love with him." Her voice conveyed how surprised she was.

After a conversation defining who he was, Patrick asked, "Does she know it?"

Dinah shook her head. "No, I don't think so. I think she believes she's finally getting over Tommy. And she prayed Patrick! She finally started talking to the Lord again." Her eyes met those of the man she had been married to for over thirty years. He read the mixture of joy and concern in her blue eyes. He reached over and grasped her hand. "All we can do is keep praying for her, Dinah." And they did.

CHAPTER 11

Jordyn was thoroughly enjoying the cool water of the pond. After going on her favorite trail, she had decided a swim and drying off in the sun sounded like heaven. As she floated with her face to the sun, she gloried in how good it felt to be there. She'd had a lot to think about after her talk with her mom. She had always wanted a relationship like her parents had. Both of her brothers were married and happily so. She was the youngest at twenty-six and already a widow. Jordyn had to admit that for a time after Tommy's death, she would never have considered marriage again. Now, after responding to something in Braeden Parker, she felt like she was moving on. Could she still find a love like the rest of her family enjoyed?

Braeden sat atop Gravity and watched Jordyn. Her boots and socks were lying haphazardly on the bank, as if she had hit the water at a run. He spied an old swinging rope and smiled. Dismounting and tethering Gravity to a nearby tree, he removed his own boots and socks.

Jordyn heard the Tarzan-like yell a split second before she felt the water surge. She sat up and looked around. Nothing. She spied Gravity tethered to a nearby tree and smiled. Braeden Parker's head suddenly emerged right in front of her.

"Hello there," she greeted the sputtering man.

"Whew! That was a little colder than I thought." The pond was fed by three springs and the water was always colder than one would expect. But if the grin on Braeden's face was any indication, he didn't mind the unexpected coolness of the water.

"I prefer to call it refreshing and relaxing."

Braeden smiled as he treaded water. "I prefer to call it fun." He turned abruptly and started swimming toward the opposite end of the large pond.

Jordyn couldn't help but laugh as she watched him play. She gave the appropriate praise when he did flips off of the gazebo that stretched into the water via a small dock. She found that she enjoyed sharing the pond with Braeden. He left her alone to float and enjoy the water, but came back every so often to let her know he hadn't forgotten she was there.

As she continued to float a respectable distance from all of the splashing, she suddenly realized how quiet it was. She sat up to see Braeden back floating not five feet from her. At least, he was trying to back float. She couldn't stop the giggle that bubbled over. He stopped rocking from side to side and sat up, smiling sheepishly.

"I never could back float. Even as a child. I'd say my Mom had to put floaties on me in the bath tub."

During their time spent together, he'd constantly referred to his family. It was nice to know that he was apparently as close to his family as she was to hers.

"I thought you said you played in the creek all day when you were a kid?"

Braeden had often told her stories of growing up on a farm and some of the exploits he and his siblings had attempted.

Braeden was now right in front of her. "We did, but we made little boats and let them go through the rapids. We only went wading in the creek to get them and only in shallow water. We weren't allowed to swim without Mom or Dad there."

"That's probably because they knew you would sink," Jordyn said teasingly.

"Haha." Braeden answered dryly.

"What do you enjoy most about sumer?"

Braeden frowned in concentration, "That's hard to say. Lightning bugs, long days, bonfires, and thunderstorms would all be on the list. What about you?"

"Water fights!" Jordyn's answer was accompanied by a large wave of water sent into Braeden's unsuspecting face. A very respectable water fight ensued.

They ended up gasping for air and laughing into each other's faces. Jordyn looked into Braeden's eyes with happiness shining in hers. She enjoyed the strength he radiated and how just being with him made her feel so...alive. Braeden's head slowly bent toward hers and her eyes instinctively slid shut.

Her eyes abruptly popped open again when instead of his lips brushing hers as she expected, his arms came around her in a tight hug. She was disappointed but after a second found herself reveling in how nice the hug felt. He held her for several minutes. He held her with a fierce intensity that told her she was cherished, special. She stared at the blue sky and enjoyed the birds, the wind chimes singing from the small gazebo, and all of the sounds of the land. To some, a kiss would have completed the picture, but both Braeden and Jordyn were enjoying the closeness they were sharing as much as the passion of a kiss. Passion would fade but relationships were built on moments like this. She sighed and closed her eyes as she rested her cheek on his right shoulder.

Braeden felt that holding Jordyn was a little slice of heaven. He'd come so close to kissing her. For a little while, he'd forgotten that he was supposed to be getting information from her, that he was here to do a job. He'd just been happy to be with her. The day couldn't have been more perfect for them. Except for the fact that he had a secret from her. Well, technically it was two secrets if you counted the fact that he had fallen in love with her, but the reason he couldn't tell her was the second secret involving his ulterior motive, so it all boiled down to one. He almost smiled at how disjointed his thoughts were getting. But it didn't change the fact that the secret was the only thing that was keeping him from pursuing a full blown romance with Jordyn. After this was over, he promised himself that he was going to explore where a relationship might lead them. If she didn't hate him by then.

"How about some lunch?"

Braeden's soft question startled Jordyn. "What?"

"Are you hungry?" Braeden asked again.

Jordyn reluctantly pulled herself from Braeden's arms. "You know, I'm actually starving."

Braeden smiled and gestured with his head toward Gravity. "Well, I've got some apples, water, trail mix bars, and some genuine store-bought brownies if you would care to partake of my humble fair."

Braeden's still pathetic Southern accent made her smile. "You really stink at that."

As he helped her onto the small dock, he adopted a hurt look. "Ah, you cut me to the quick." He said as he put a hand to his heart and then adopted a pouting expression. "Maybe I don't want to share my food now."

His pouting was too cute. A hungry Jordyn instantly put on an apologetic and very serious look. "If I offended you, I'm deeply sorry. I'll do whatever I can to make up for my lack of sensitivity."

Hmm...Braeden rubbed his chin in an attitude of deep contemplation. "Do you really mean it or are you just hungry?"

"Oh, I mean it. I really do." She innocently batted her eyelashes at him.

He nodded decisively. "Okay. Have dinner with me tomorrow night and I'll forgive you."

Jordyn was surprised. "We've been having dinner together almost every night."

"I know but I want to take you somewhere special." Braeden's look was so hopeful that Jordyn smiled. She didn't know how but he always made her feel so special.

"I would love to. Where would you like to go?"

Braeden shook his head. "Oh no. It's going to be a surprise."

Jordyn decided to try and wheedle it out of him. "How will I know what I need to wear?"

Braeden thought about that for a second. "I'll be wearing khakis, a light blue button-down, and a sport coat. You'll just have to judge by what I'm wearing."

"I appreciate that information, but now you've got me curious. Where would we go that you would feel the need to wear a sport coat?"

Braeden remained stubbornly silent. Jordyn cocked her head to one side in a questioning gesture. She laughed aloud when Braeden mimicked the movement.

"Are you sure you don't want to tell me?"

"No can do. You'll have to find out tomorrow. And I don't mean when we're working tomorrow so don't even try to get it out of me. You'll find out sometime after I pick you up at six forty-five."

They spent the rest of the afternoon, eating lunch, drying in the sun, and talking and laughing about everything. That evening they checked the traps, which were empty. They still enjoyed the ride to the traps and back to the house though. It was as if both of them realized that these days together were special and should be enjoyed to the fullest.

CHAPTER 12

Monica sighed with worry as she listened to Jordyn's account of her afternoon with Braeden, minus the rather disconcerting hug. Monica was so lost in her own thoughts about how to get Jordyn to slow down when she heard her say, "And I think Dave disapproves of Braeden."

Monica's interest was piqued at that comment. "Why would you say that?"

Jordyn's voice turned a bit dry. "Because he didn't stop glaring at Braeden from the time we rode in together, and he didn't offer to take care of Phantom for me like he normally does."

"Well, maybe he has good instincts." Monica really hated how that sounded.

There was a pause before Jordyn asked, "And how would you know that his instincts about Braeden are good? You've only seen Braeden once before and you've never talked to him."

"I have good instincts too and I trust Dave." Monica knew how ridiculous that sounded and couldn't help it. It would hurt Jordyn to tell her the truth, the whole truth, and nothing but the truth. So, she was trying to encourage Jordyn to keep Braeden at arm's length. You could enjoy a date at arm's length couldn't you?

"Okay, Mon, what gives?" The confusion Jordyn was feeling was evident in the frustration behind the question.

"I don't know what you mean." Monica said evasively.

"Yes, you do. A few days ago you were pushing me to go for Braeden and now you sound like you don't trust him." Jordyn paused. "Level with me, Mon. What are you not telling me that you really want to say?"

Monica closed her eyes and rubbed her left temple. "I just don't want you to get into a serious relationship and get hurt."

"You mean like I did with Tommy."

"I didn't say that, Jordyn." She paused as she groped for the right words. "Honey, I know something has made you grieve for Tommy beyond what I would have expected." Monica found herself struggling for words. She finally decided to be as honest as she could.

"You've never talked much about Tommy after his death. Or before for that matter. Even to Faith and I. I don't expect you to tell us everything about your life, but clearly something happened that's still bothering you. I don't want you carrying that pain around. In regard to Braeden Parker, I don't think you're in a position to begin a new relationship without laying Tommy to rest once and for all."

Jordyn's eyes stung a bit at the truth of Monica's words. She did feel like she was beginning to live again, but she still had a long way to go. "Thank you for being honest with me." Monica groaned inwardly at that. "And thanks for your concern."

Jordyn sighed as she reflected on what she should do. "You're right. There are some things I hesitated to tell you about Tommy. If you and Faith are free for lunch tomorrow, I think its past time we had a long talk."

Monica didn't think she could feel guiltier as she said, "Any time you're ready, tomorrow or next year, we will be there to listen." She kept trying to tell herself that she was interested as a friend more than anything.

"Thanks, Mon. I'll see ya here at twelve-thirty."

"Okay, see you."

As the connection was broken, Jordyn felt relief at deciding to tell her friends the truth about her marriage. On the other hand, the conversation had caused her to second guess her relationship with Braeden Parker. He knew more about her and Tommy than Faith and Monica. Was that why he hesitated to kiss her? Was he afraid that she wasn't ready for a romantic relationship and was trying to protect her from herself? She didn't think so in light of the fact that he'd invited her out for dinner. After considering all she knew about Braeden, she decided that Mon was being overly cautious. Monica just didn't know Braeden like she did. He wouldn't do anything to hurt her. She had a feeling that he would do all he could to protect her.

Her phone interrupted her musings. The caller ID said unavailable again. She figured she would answer it and tell them to stop calling.

"Hello."

"Put the papers in your mailbox tomorrow night and make sure everyone is gone."

"Who is this?" Jordyn didn't know how she pushed the words past the sudden dryness of her throat.

All she heard in answer to her question was silence. Jordyn had no idea what they were talking about. Her mind ran the gamut of possibilities. Maybe they had gotten the wrong number. Maybe it was a prank, but she didn't think so. People who made demands such as that didn't accidentally call the wrong number. And she had been half expecting something like this to happen. There were too many unexplained things happening and too many secrets in Tommy's past.

She sat for a moment and then started to call Braeden. She stopped. Monica's warning about pushing their relationship too fast rang in her ears. She sank into one of the large leather couches in the living room, her mind racing despite the heaviness of her limbs.

They wanted papers. What papers could anyone want from here? "Oh Lord, I need you to help me think clearly and not in a cloud of fear." The only thing of interest on Promise Land would appeal to biologists and other researchers, but not people who would threaten her to get them. It had to be something that involved Tommy, but she really had no clue what it would be.

She was genuinely frightened. The caller hadn't explicitly threatened her, but it hadn't been necessary. They, whoever they were, clearly thought she knew that she had something that they wanted. Since she had no clue what that might be, she would have to start looking for what that was.

Three hours later, she was staring at an old cell phone bill that she couldn't believe she still had. She had been through every file of the farm records for the last five years. She had come up blank. Fearing what she might find, she had moved to her personal papers. The phone bill was filled with a list of normal phone calls. And several from an unavailable number. She looked at the receiving number. It was what she expected. It was Tommy's number.

"Oh Lord, I don't know what this means. I'm scared that Tommy was into something. What do I do Lord? Please, please…" She didn't even know what to ask for, but she knew the Lord knew exactly what she needed.

She jumped when her cell phone started yelling at her to answer Monica.

"Hello."

"Hey, are you okay? You sound a bit strained."

"Oh, no." Jordyn cringed at the partial lie. She wasn't strained, she was terrified. "I'm going through old papers and I hate it, so I'm a tad grouchy."

"Well, I hope this doesn't make it worse, but Faith can't make it tomorrow afternoon. It's her Mom's birthday and the family is spending the day together. How about Wednesday?"

"Wednesday sounds good." *If I'm still alive*, Jordyn added silently. "I'll see you then."

Jordyn sat in her father's big desk chair and thought the situation through, praying about what she should do. She remembered telling Monica months ago that she felt like someone was watching her. Since then, she had felt odd if the shades were open after dark, and a bit uncomfortable if she went outside after dark. Rafe's call about Tommy's car had added to her already growing suspicion. Now she was pretty sure that the spliced fence was definitely not a fluke. Whatever was going on, she needed to figure it out and soon. Sometime around 1:00 a.m., she came to a decision. She searched through the rest of the cell phone records and made copies. Then she highlighted every unavailable phone call, noticing that they came with increasing regularity the week of Tommy's death. She paper clipped them together, stuffed them in a manila envelope, and set them on the kitchen counter. As she headed to bed, she passed the security system board. For the first time in a long time, she tested and then set the alarm.

Monica stared at the phone. Jordyn was not all right. Something was upsetting her. For an instant, Monica was afraid their conversation was the culprit. But Jordyn had sounded fine when she hung up after setting their lunch date—relieved even. It was something else. Braeden hadn't been there, but Jordyn seemed okay with that after their day together.

Monica sat bolt upright. Jordyn had said she was going through old papers. Had she found something Tommy left? Would he have been dumb enough to keep them with all of the rest of their papers? Monica decided that he wouldn't have, but you never know. The best hiding places are sometimes right in the open. It was eleven-thirty. She would call Luke in the morning and see what he thought she should do. She would almost call Jordyn back, but didn't have a specific reason to. How could she find out what, if anything, Jordyn had found? How could she ever explain things to Jordyn if it came to that?

CHAPTER 13

The next day found Jordyn talking to Dave in not so quiet tones. "I want you to go today, Dave. Take Corey and Neal and see if you can't help them out for a little while. They need it."

Dave was shaking his head. "I don't understand why you have a burning desire for us to go help repair the camp when no one will be here to help you."

"I can hire a day hand from my church if I need to. I'm sure Pastor Charles could recommend several to keep up the basic chores and I can handle everything else. Besides, it's not like you would be gone forever. And I'll have Braeden here in case of an emergency." Jordyn was getting desperate to make him leave. She had come to the conclusion last night that a trip was the only way to get her three hands off of the ranch this evening. It just wasn't going as smoothly as she'd hoped.

"Dave, that camp has needed repairs for a long time and after that last bad storm, Pastor Charles says that it's not even in working order. Please? Do this for me?"

Dave stared at Jordyn hard. He had known her all of her life and he knew there was a reason behind this that she wasn't telling him. "Okay, if it's that important to you, we'll head out in the morning."

"Actually, I was thinking that you guys should go to Pigeon Forge this evening and spend the night. On me. Have some fun tomorrow. Drive through Cades Cove or go fishing or something. Then you guys can head out the day after tomorrow."

Dave frowned but knew that he was going to lose this argument. "If that's what you want."

Two hours later, Dave, Corey, and Neal headed down the long drive. Jordyn watched them go and then looked around. She felt like there were eyes everywhere now. And she'd never felt so completely alone.

Jordyn had dressed for the date carefully. The forest green dress had been a favorite since she had bought it on one of her last visits to the Big Apple. Her hair was in a French twist with loose tendrils framing her face. She was excited about their date and was looking forward to a wonderful evening. Her eyes strayed to the kitchen counter. Who was she kidding? The last thing she was going to be able to do was have a nice evening knowing that someone was lurking around her mailbox and possibly her home.

The copied phone records were there. Black ink blocked out any information she wished to conceal. The yellow highlighted unavailable calls were the only thing legible on the sheets. On the top sheet she had written, "What papers do you want?"

She had considered calling the police, but had decided against it. What if Tommy had been into something illegal? She would try to protect her family name from the repercussions of that no matter the cost.

She had checked the alarm on the front gate and reset the code. She had done the same for the house and barns. There was a small automatic pistol in her purse. As she placed the gun into the bag, she reflected on how surreal it felt in her hand. She put her cell phone in next to the gun. She had made sure it was charged and kept it with her all day. She had a feeling she would get a call when they found the note she left.

The knock on the door made her jump slightly. *Braeden.* That's the only person it could be since she had sent all three of her hired hands to do repairs on the summer camp owned by her church. They hadn't been happy about her signing them up, but they couldn't object to the cause. Besides, she felt better knowing that they were going to be gone for a few days. She sent a prayer heavenward that she would be able to keep it together this evening. She grabbed the stack of papers off of the counter and headed toward the front door.

Braeden smiled at how beautiful Jordyn looked. The dress accented her hair and eyes. And knocked his socks off. She smiled her welcome a bit nervously and asked, "Do you want some coffee or something before we go?"

"No, I'm afraid we will be late if we do that."

Jordyn gave a small shrug. "Well, I'm ready if you are."

Braeden surprised her by handing her a miniature vase with miniature roses in it. The gift was unique, just like Braeden. When she looked up, he leaned in and planted a soft kiss on her lips. He hesitated, holding his lips above hers before finally moving back.

"Thank you," she said a bit breathlessly.

Braeden grinned teasingly. "For the roses or the kiss."

"Both."

He stepped back and waited for her to precede him out of the house. She smiled and shook her head. "I need to go last so I can set the alarm."

Braeden stepped onto the porch and waited. After she set the alarm, they headed to her car. As he helped her into the passenger side he said, "I hope you don't mind your date using your car. I didn't think you wanted to go on a date in my truck."

"I wouldn't have minded."

Braeden looked at her and said sincerely, "I know. That's one of the reasons I like you so well."

As he said this, he reached for her hand. To her surprise, she was enjoying holding his hand so much she almost forgot to ask him to stop at the mailbox. At her request, he looked at her quizzically but stopped without asking any questions. He reached for the papers and put them in the box for her. She hoped he hadn't noticed the lack of address and that he wouldn't ask any questions. He put the flag up and walked back to the car. No such luck. As soon as he got back in the car and put it in gear he asked, "Do you want to tell me what that was about?"

"I just wanted to make sure that got sent out." She was fairly certain she sounded normal. "The people who need that information are anxious to get it." That was the truth at least. As they pulled from her drive onto the main road, she used a remote to set the lock on the front gate. At his questioning glance, she said cheerfully, "I'm looking forward to finding out where we're going!"

Braeden smiled as he pulled onto the main road. If she didn't want to talk about whatever was bothering her that was fine for now. "Well, I'm not going to tell you. You'll find out when we get there." He flicked on her stereo to hear Frank's voice crooning "Under My Skin." How suitable, Braeden thought ironically.

Jordyn was glad for the lack of conversation in the car. She couldn't get her mind to stop wishing she could keep an eye on her mailbox. In reality though, it was best that she didn't. She felt a bit of hysterical laughter about to bubble over as she pictured herself hanging out in the brush for most of the night, Nancy Drew style, trying to spy on her own mailbox. As they headed toward Gatlinburg and made a turn up a mountain road, Jordyn forgot about her problem and began to pay more attention.

When they cruised into the parking lot, Jordyn couldn't believe her eyes. The restaurant had been strategically placed at the top of the mountain, commanding a truly awesome view.

"Look at that view!" She said with more than a little awe.

Braeden smiled. "It's awesome, isn't it?"

"You can see for miles. It's the best view I've seen around here."

"That's where the restaurant gets its name." Braeden gestured to a sign tastefully designed as a placard "The View."

"Oh I've heard about this place! It's the restaurant at the top of Sky Mountain! Monica, Faith, and I were going to come for lunch a few weeks ago but it was booked." Jordyn glanced at Braeden. "How did you get us in on such short notice? You just asked me about dinner yesterday."

Braeden smiled smugly. "I'm very important in certain circles."

At Jordyn's raised eyebrow he said, "Okay. I had a buddy in college who I helped with some homework. He used to work at Cade's Cove. A few years ago, it was discovered that his great-aunt, whom none of them knew much about, left Sky Mountain to the youngest male in her family. That just so happened to be him. He built about two dozen cabins on the mountain and this restaurant. He's left the rest untouched." Braeden stood in the parking lot looking through the arches that led to a patio on the other side. There was a small garden area that led to a sheer cliff. Beyond the cliff was one of the most beautiful views in the world. The Smoky Mountains in all of their glory rose in blue bulk reaching for the sky. No traffic or modern buildings marred the view of rugged wilderness. It was truly awe-inspiring. "I don't think he'll do anything to spoil that."

Braeden led her into a reception area that housed a comfortable seating area for those waiting for a table. Huge log pillars supported the floor above and a large desk housed the hostess with two staircases on each side leading up to the dining room above. When Braeden gave his name, a hostess smiled and immediately asked them to follow her.

She led them up the staircase on the left side of the desk. They walked into a huge dining area, with tables filled to capacity with diners. Huge fireplaces dominated the walls and the chandeliers flickered with real candles. The main attraction was the floor to ceiling windows that commanded a front row seat to see the setting sun.

Jordyn was taking it all in with much appreciation. She'd been to some of the best restaurants in New York where expensive elegance was the thing. However, this restaurant was built around the beauty of God's creation. After they reached the dining area, the hostess led them around the corner and up another large staircase. The huge double doors at the top were closed but the hostess swiped her card and the big doors unlocked. She held the door and motioned to a table directly in the center of the large windows. Like the floor below the windows in the smaller dining area were from floor to ceiling. However, you couldn't see the patio from this level because the balcony-like room jutted out further than the floor below. All a diner could see was the late evening sun turning the sky a dozen different shades of red, gold, and pink. The mountains looked even bluer than usual, almost purple with sporadic jagged rock cliffs turned to gold by the sun's rays. The fireplaces on both sides of the room were lit, adding a comforting crackle and glow to the room. The candles on every table and the chandeliers gave off enough light to make the polished wood floor look like molten gold. Even the wall sconces held lit candles. Small electric lights strategically placed on the underside of the hip-high chair rail kept the room well lit without spoiling the atmosphere.

Jordyn looked at Braeden's expectant expression after the hostess disappeared and said, "It's perfect."

"I'm glad you like it." He had been out to impress her and he had succeeded.

Jordyn looked around at all of the empty tables. "I can't believe we're the only people up here."

"I asked Clayton how busy he was this time of year. I told him I had a date with the elusive Ms. Grey and we wanted some privacy. He said he didn't usually open this floor until later in the evening anyway." Braeden smiled at her obvious delight over their dinner accommodations. "There's a photographer here doing pictures for a new brochure too. We can get our picture made on the way out and the charity board will be happy."

"You've thought of everything." Jordyn couldn't believe how much all of the trouble he had gone to meant to her.

"I surely tried to, ma'am," Braeden said in his bad Southern drawl that always made her laugh.

Their waiter appeared and took their drink order. As he disappeared out a door that Jordyn hadn't even noticed, she realized that she couldn't hear the diners below. There was also soft music playing. Jordyn couldn't think of anything that would make this evening more perfect.

Braeden broke into her thoughts. "What would you like to order?" he asked as he pursued his menu.

Jordyn studied the many options before cocking an eyebrow at Braeden. "What would you recommend?"

Braeden shrugged one broad shoulder. "I like the filet mignon, but everything on the menu is good."

Jordyn nodded. "I think I'll have the same then."

"Good choice. That's one of my favorites." Braeden raised an eyebrow over the appetizers. "Do you see anything else you want?"

Jordyn stared at the menu. It all sounded delicious, but she wasn't sure the butterflies in her stomach would settle long enough for her to eat her meal much less an appetizer. "I think we should save room for a dessert."

Braeden smiled. "Was that a hint?"

"I've never shared a dessert with a date and I'd like to give it a try." Jordyn smiled slyly. "Any objections?"

"No, ma'am," was Braeden's quick response.

As if on cue, their waiter appeared with their drinks and took their order. After he left, Braeden nodded to the empty balcony. "Care to? I'm sure the view will be most inspiring."

Jordyn wouldn't let herself reflect on the fact that he considered this an honest to goodness date and smiled at his discomfort. "I'd love to go enjoy the view with you."

Braeden rose and moved to help her out of her chair. As they wove their way toward the balcony, he grasped her hand, entwining their fingers. Jordyn couldn't help but look at the strong masculine hand holding hers. For some reason, the mixture of strength and tenderness in the touch of his hand made her eyes tear up. It felt good to relax and let someone else worry about her for a change. Even if it was only for an evening.

When she started to sit down in one of the many chairs, Braeden stopped her. "Hang on a second." He whipped out a handkerchief and wiped it off then looked up at her and winked. "I wouldn't want my date to get her beautiful dress dirty."

Jordyn laughed at his expression. He was entirely too pleased with himself. "Are you always this chivalrous on dates?"

"I hope so because my Mom would have a fit if she thought I wasn't. She has very definite ideas about how a young man should treat his lady."

Jordyn really liked being called his lady. "Oh, really. Like what?"

"Well, I'd say we were the only boys in school to go last in the lunch line so we didn't get in front of a girl. We didn't want to tell Mom that we hadn't adhered to the ladies first rule."

Jordyn laughed. "She did a good job."

"She thinks so. She's the gentlest person I know. And in many ways she's the strongest. And she was as tough on Bailey as she was on Brock and I. I think Bailey was the only girl who never called her high school sweetheart. Mom didn't think a young lady should call a guy."

Jordyn laughed. "Oh, your Mom wouldn't have liked it at our house."

Braeden smiled. "Kept the lines busy did you?"

"Not me," Jordyn answered quickly, "but my brothers were always being called to the phone by their latest crush."

"Well, Bailey's none the worse for wear. She learned that relationships are important and not an accessory to high school. In a way, Mom was demanding that she respect the boys as much as she demanded their respect for her little girl."

"What's Bailey doing now?"

Braeden's love and pride shone in his smiling eyes. "She's twenty-six and is working on a tourist brochure issued by the state of Virginia. She's a very gifted photographer." He smiled wryly. "She's also engaged to her high school sweetheart so I guess Mom knew what she was doing."

They danced on in silence and Jordyn couldn't believe how good it felt to be in his arms. As she had listened to him talk about his family, she realized how much she cared for everything about Braeden. Too soon or not, she was head over heels for Braeden Parker. She wanted to tell him how much he meant to her, but subconsciously the memory of her life with Tommy and her current situation kept her quiet.

Her eyes must have said what her mouth could not however, because he lowered his lips to hers. At first tentative, the kiss became the words that neither felt they could say. As he drew back after tilting her world, Jordyn let her head fall to his shoulder. It felt so right to be in his arms. It felt safe. And exciting.

Braeden forgot about his job and his feelings of guilt. At that moment, all that mattered was Jordyn. He loved her. Hopeless though it was, he still loved her. And for now, he was going to concentrate on the present and not worry about the past or the future.

After the dance, they ate dinner. The food was delicious and the atmosphere romantic. They talked about their dreams. Jordyn wanted to do charity work and Braeden wanted a full-time position managing a place like Promise Land. They loved God, their families, and their country. They loved Andy Griffith and country drives. They both wanted two kids.

"So, what was it like to grow up with two older brothers?" Braeden asked.

Jordyn laughed. "At times it was very frustrating. When I was little, they never wanted me to tag along because I couldn't keep up. When I got older, they didn't want me to go on fishing trips and such because I always beat them. By the time I started dating, they felt like it was their duty to scare of any unsuitable suitors, which was all of them."

"So, you would rather have a sister."

Jordyn smiled. "Not in a million years would I trade my overbearing and wonderful older brothers for a silly sister. Once we figured out how to live in harmony, we became the best of friends." Jordyn's eyes twinkled over her water goblet. "I even picked their wives."

This comment caused Braeden to sputter as he was attempting a drink. "You picked out who your brothers married?" He shook his head. "I love my sister but I do have limits."

"Well, I say I picked them, but it's more like I introduced them. I worked with Kyle's wife during an internship in college at a charity organization to aid the blind. I thought she was one of the sweetest people I'd ever met and perfect for my older brother. I invited her to a Grey Foundation cookout and the rest is history."

"So, she works for a charity?"

"Sort of. She is a consultant for setting up events for the recipients of the organization. She's been blind since being in a car accident when she was five."

Braeden smiled. "She sounds like a special lady."

Jordyn smiled impishly. "She is. She's given me two beautiful nephews to spoil. That rates her pretty high in my book."

Braeden laughed easily. "And your other brother's wife hasn't done that yet?"

"Nope. Maggie and Jack are both too busy to have kids right now. She's a lawyer and he helps Dad with the family business. They keep telling us someday though."

"And how did you meet Maggie?" Braeden asked.

"Actually, Monica introduced us. Maggie was at Harvard the same time as Mon."

Braeden seemed surprised. "Monica went to Harvard?"

Jordyn smiled. "I know it sounds odd if you've never met her. She doesn't seem the bookish sort, but she actually has her doctorate in political science."

Braeden was shaking his head in genuine wonder at Jordyn's odd friend when she asked him a question he wasn't prepared to answer. "So, what does Brock do?"

Braeden felt his heart jump and he almost jerked the hand that had found Jordyn's away. How could he answer that honestly? "He's a government employee." He hoped his voice didn't portray the tension in his stomach.

Jordyn cocked her head to the side and grinned at him. "That was specific."

Her questioning sarcasm wasn't lost on Braeden and his smile was not as sure as it had been earlier. "Well, I can't exactly give specifics for what Brock does." Sensing an avenue of escape, Braeden went on hurriedly. "To be honest, I don't even know all of the specifics of what he does." That was true. He knew generally that Brock was a U.S. Marshal and that he handled witnesses frequently. How exactly he did his job Braeden had no idea.

"So, he's definitely not a postal worker." Jordyn stated it but Braeden could still hear the question.

"Nope. He's a U.S. Marshal and that's really all I can say." Braeden hoped she wouldn't press the issue.

"I didn't know that being a U.S. Marshal was such a big deal. I would expect this kind of covertness to be involved with the CIA or something." Jordyn's soft chuckle made him feel as if he'd overdone the secrecy aspect of his brother's job. In ordinary circumstances, he'd be able to tell Jordyn that Brock handled many things, including being a handler for the witness protection program.

He sighed heavily. "I know. I just think it's cool to have a brother who is a federal agent. I tend to blow it out of proportion sometimes." He grinned and then adopted a pitiful look. "It makes what I do seem so tame."

Jordyn laughed at the look of utter despair on Braeden's face. "I don't think anyone would consider working with wild animals a tame profession, even your hotshot brother."

"I never said that he was a hotshot federal agent. Just that he is a federal agent. If you go and make him sound like James Bond, you're going to deflate my fragile ego."

Jordyn laughed at the ridiculous notion. Braeden was as proud of his older brother as he was of Bailey and it showed. Jordyn had a feeling that his two siblings were probably as proud of him as he was of them.

They continued to talk about their family, their dreams, and their plans for the rest of the evening.

CHAPTER 14

The flow of conversation established during their date didn't stop as they drove home. Both felt as if they had known the other for years instead of a few months. The bubble of happiness was burst when they pulled up to the gate of Promise Land. Something was very wrong if the flashing blue and red lights were any indication. The gate was open so Braeden stepped on the accelerator and made it to the house in record time.

Jordyn stared at the number of police cars, fire trucks, and ambulances that surrounded her once peaceful abode. She got out of the car without waiting for Braeden to open the door and started running toward the house. Braeden caught up with her when she was stopped by a young officer standing at the bottom of the porch steps.

"Excuse me ma'am, but I can't let you go in."

Jordyn jerked her arm free. "But it's my house!" she insisted.

Braeden stepped up and placed both hands on her shoulders. "Let them do their job, Jordyn." His voice was calm and reasonable. He slipped out of his jacket and slipped it onto Jordyn's shaking shoulders. He turned to the officer. "We will be in the car when someone needs to speak with Ms. Grey."

After they settled back into the car, Jordyn sat in silence for a few minutes before she asked, "What has happened?" Her voice sounded so hallow that Braeden felt a growing concern.

"It looks like a burglary. The house seems to be where everybody is congregating. It's not on fire and I haven't seen any ambulances leave, so it's not life threatening." He studied her face and was very glad she hadn't been there. "At least you were gone."

Jordyn nodded absently and watched as officers and crime scene technicians bustled about doing their respective tasks. It felt like hours had passed instead of minutes and Jordyn felt like she was going to burst with impatience when two officers finally approached the car.

The tall, thin one said, "Excuse me. Are you Ms. Grey?"

At Jordyn's nod the short, stocky officer said, "We would like to speak with you before you see the house if you don't mind." Without waiting for her response as she and Braeden got out of the car he continued, "I'm Detective Anderson and this is Detective Boyd."

Detective Boyd pulled out a small notebook. "Where were you this evening, Ms. Grey?" His tone wasn't unkind, but it wouldn't have won an award for Sunshine Officer of the Month either.

"I was at dinner with Dr. Braeden Parker. He's here doing research on our current wolf population."

Braeden couldn't help but notice how most of her answer involved him and very little about her.

Detective Boyd's eyes went from one to the other. "Did anyone know you were going to be away from the house this evening?"

Jordyn shrugged. "One of my friends, Monica Wallace, is the only person I told." Jordyn cringed as she realized that was a bit misleading. She knew that someone else had known she wouldn't be home. Was it a lie if she didn't know who it was? Anyway, telling the detectives about her situation probably wouldn't help it any.

"Dr. Parker,"—Detective Anderson turned to Braeden—"did you tell anyone that both you and Ms. Grey were going to be gone tonight?"

"No," Braeden thought he knew who was responsible though.

The detective apparently decided that Braeden wasn't important and turned back to Jordyn. "Can you think of anybody that has a grudge against you personally?"

Angela Beaumont was the only person Jordyn had really made mad lately. Somehow, she didn't think that Angela would have done whatever the police weren't telling her about. Besides, she was willing to bet that the mailbox was empty and that her question hadn't made the recipient very happy.

"We've never had anything like this happen before." Jordyn gave the detective a classic nonanswer. "We've never even had petty theft let alone robbery."

The detectives exchanged glances. It didn't take a genius to figure out that something wasn't right.

"What's the problem?" Braeden's question was sharp and got both detectives' attention.

"It doesn't appear to be a burglary. At least, not that we can tell. The art wasn't taken, the antique book collection wasn't even touched." Detective Anderson's eyes swung to Jordyn. "It's almost like they were looking for something specific."

Jordyn shook her head. "If they weren't interested in burglarizing the house then they had to be interested in our files. Only researchers or an environmental protest group would be interested in those."

Detective Boyd asked, "What makes you think they were looking for papers?"

Jorydn shrugged. "You said that they weren't interested in art or anything valuable. Our files are the only other thing of interest in the house." Jordyn's quick answer seemed to satisfy the terminal suspicion for everyone except Braeden. For the first time in the months they'd spent together, Braeden was beginning to think that Jordyn might know something she would be better off not knowing about.

"Well, we need to make sure nothing is missing"— Detective Anderson gestured toward the house—"if you don't mind checking."

Jordyn nodded and stepped toward the house. She felt close to tears when Braeden's strong masculine hand grasped hers and squeezed. She drew comfort from that simple squeeze.

Detective Anderson stopped at the door. "You might want to prepare yourself. They worked the place over pretty thoroughly."

Jordyn nodded and took a deep breath, squeezing Braeden's hand. When she stepped through the door, she was glad she had his hand. She reeled from the shock of seeing her childhood home in shambles. She wouldn't have recognized it if someone had taken a picture and showed it to her. The table in the foyer had been smashed. The mirror was shattered and tiny shards of glass covered the floor like sparkling silver. The two huge couches in the living room had been overturned and slashed, along with all of the chairs. There was not one painting left on the walls. All of the frames had been broken. Not one item had been left unscathed. As they walked past the den that doubled as the library, she noticed that a portrait of her father seated in front of the fireplace with Riley, the family's Doberman, had been mutilated beyond recognition. All of the books were in the floor. Some of them had pages torn out. But almost to make a point, the valuable antique book collection had been left searched but undamaged.

As they entered the study room that doubled as her office for Promise Land, she felt the first twinges of anger. It had clearly received the worst of the onslaught. Papers were strewn from one end to the other. The oak filing cabinets had been beaten into pieces. The desk, her great-grandfather's desk, had no legs. Tears filled her eyes as she ran her hand over the wood. When she was little, she used to see how much she had grown by standing beside the desk and marking the smooth, polished side with chalk. This wasn't just a violation of property. It was a violation on her memories of her home. The desk chair had been thrown out the bay window and the cool night air meandering in was refreshing to the distraught Jordyn.

"We believe that the demolition, for lack of a better word, started here," said Detective Anderson. His voice held more than a little sympathy. "As you can see, this room has the most damage. We think whoever did this was looking for something they expected to find in here or in the previous two rooms because the kitchen and dining room are relatively untouched compared to this."

Jordyn dreaded looking at the rest of the house, but she headed down the east hallway which housed the master suite and the other six suites in the house. As she passed the door to each room she looked in, the bedrooms weren't in as bad as shape as the study, den, and living room. In one room, there was still a landscape hanging on the wall, but the sky was now tilted way too far west. Jordyn gave it a grim look. That's how she felt, like her world was being knocked off kilter.

As she reached the door to the master suite, her room, she prepared herself for a scenario as bad as the rest of the rooms. She stepped into the room and stopped. She blinked several times before looking questioningly at the detectives who were waiting for her reaction.

"It stumped us too," said Detective Anderson. "Either this room was searched by one individual who didn't participate in searching the rest of the house, or they're trying to send you some type of message." He paused a moment before adding, "Which would imply that they know you."

Jordyn stared at her neat room. She could hardly tell that anyone had been in here. Her clothes in her closet were mussed and there was a sock toe sticking out of her dresser. Other than that, it was just as she had left it. She felt a chill when she realized that if the rest of the house hadn't been such a disaster, she wouldn't have noticed the differences.

"What message are they trying to send here?" Braeden asked.

"Well, our forensic psychologist said that the bedroom being so neat is a mind game. They can make it obvious that they're here only if they want to." Detective Boyd paused. "But that's not the real problem." He turned back to Jordyn. "How do you open the gate?"

Jordyn shrugged. "Any intercom in the house can do it. All you have to do is push the gate button." When Detective Boyd smacked his notebook into the palm of the other hand in clear frustration Jordyn asked, "Why?"

"Because whoever did this, let us in." At Jordyn's sharp intake of breath he continued, "They also called 911."

"Hold on a minute"—Braeden cut in sharply—"are you telling me that whoever did all of this bypassed a high security system, called the police, and stayed here long enough to let them in?" His voice showed his disbelief and horror at the thought.

"I'm afraid so." Detective Anderson gestured to the phone on Jordyn's nightstand. "And they called from right there. It's the only phone in the house that still works."

Jordyn tried swallowing and if felt like she had a mouth full of flour. She finally got her question out. "Are you sure the security company didn't open the gate? They can do that from their office once the alarm is activated."

Detective Anderson shook his head and answered with no small amount of sympathy now, "No, the call came from here and the gate was opened from this control."

Everyone stared at the indention on the neatly made up bed. Jordyn felt sick. Whoever had done this had sat on her bed, called the police, and waited until they arrived.

Braeden ran a hand through his hair in a gesture of agitation that Jordyn had never seen before. "Did the police see anybody leaving when they got here?"

"Our first responding officers swept the house before backup ever got here. No one has seen anything or anybody that looked suspicious."

Braeden knew what this was. It was a message. The message was telling Jordyn that she wasn't safe, even in her own home. Apparently, everybody thought she knew what the papers were and where they were hidden. As he studied her face, he was afraid they were right. And the fact that he hadn't seen it before bothered him.

"Are there any indications that they found what they were looking for?" Jordyn's question fell into a silence.

"No," answered both detectives simultaneously.

"Jordyn!" The shout came from the porch. Without so much as a glance at all of the destruction, Monica ran in and hugged Jordyn.

"Honey, are you okay? Please tell me you weren't here when this happened."

Jordyn smiled tremulously. "I just found out about it a little while ago. The police were here before I was. How'd you find out?"

Monica waved a hand in the air as if to pass it off. "That's not important. I'm here to help you with anything and I want you to come home with me."

"If you don't mind ma'am, I would like to know how you found out about this. I think it would be in Ms. Grey's best interest not to make this public knowledge." Detective Anderson's voice was quiet, but authoritative.

Monica gave him a level look. "Our cook's son is a state trooper. She listens to her police scanner more religiously than most women her age watch soaps." She gave a little shrug and her answer seemed to satisfy that it hadn't been in the eleven o'clock news.

Monica turned back to Jordyn. "I'll help you pack up some things and we will stay at Dad's cabin tonight."

Jordyn was about to protest when Braeden stepped forward and grasped her shoulders. "Jordyn, I know you feel like you're giving them the field by leaving, but I think it's the best thing you could do for tonight." He let this sink in. "I'll be in the apartment and tomorrow we will get the security system checked out and get the house cleaned up. Just go with Monica tonight, okay?"

Jordyn nodded and Braeden pulled her into a tight hug. He had to get this resolved before Jordyn ended up like Tommy.

As Jordyn turned to go, Detective Anderson stopped her. "There's one more thing, Ms. Grey. Whoever did this knew what they were doing. It takes a professional to know how to bypass a security system as sophisticated as yours." He paused and his own frustration at the situation came through. "Whoever called us sat on your bed and watched the police pull up to the gate and then opened it for them. These people feel they are above the law. They aren't afraid of getting caught. They aren't afraid of the police. I'm not trying to scare you, ma'am, but I think these people are the kind that play for keeps."

Jordyn looked at Braeden. "It might not be safe for you to stay either."

"I think I'll be fine. The barns weren't touched. Besides, I need to be here to check the traps."

Jordyn nodded slowly, but it was clear she didn't like the situation.

"I'll be back first thing tomorrow morning," she said.

"I'll be here," Braeden said as he squeezed the hand he was holding. And didn't want to let go of. He could tell that her thoughts were mirroring his own. Their perfect dinner, their dance, and their feelings were only made even clearer by the intimation of danger.

As Monica and Jordyn headed off to gather some clothes for Jordyn, Braeden turned toward his temporary apartment home. Before he was halfway there, his cell phone was pressed to his ear. His call was answered on the first ring.

"We heard, Braeden. The FBI had a team watching the house. They saw three men enter and notified their contact. She should be there by now. Apparently, everybody is in full cooperation."

"I haven't seen any FBI agent, but it's a bit of a zoo here at the moment." Braeden couldn't believe how calmly he was carrying on this conversation. The fact that they had gotten so close to Jordyn, so close to her sanctuary scared him.

"She's undercover too, a personal friend of Jordyn's it seems. Not exactly an agent."

That bit of information brought Braeden up short. So, that fortuitous timing of Monica's wasn't a coincidence. At least Jordyn was going to be with someone who had a gun and cared about her. The only thing better would involve him being her personal bodyguard on a military installation somewhere in Alaska.

"She could've been killed tonight, Brock." Saying the words aloud made Braeden's voice rough, uneven.

There was a pause then, "Are you too close to this?"

Braeden seriously considered the question. "I don't think so. I just don't like seeing her as a sitting duck for whoever decides to try for her." He paused before he added, "I've come to care about her a great deal."

"Then you can rest easier. The FBI seems to have a constant eye on her, except when she's with you in the wilds of Tennessee. They saw three men enter the house by the front door and three men leave via the kitchen patio door. She wasn't in any real danger. They would have stopped her from going into the house if her visitors had still been there."

Braeden trusted this man. They were brothers after all. But he didn't know if he could trust him with Jordyn's life. Not that Brock would let him down. He cared for all of his cases far too much. But this was about Jordyn.

"Braeden, I know you've developed deep feelings for Jordyn Grey." Brock paused and for the first time Braeden realized how hard it was for him as well. "Do you think she knows anything?"

Braeden sighed heavily. "Yes. I put a pack of papers in the mailbox that didn't have a stamp on the envelope. She normally sends stuff UPS. She acted nervous about it and she set the alarm before we left tonight. I've never seen her do that before." He ran frustrated fingers through his mussed hair. "I'm not sure what she knows, but she does know something."

Braeden felt that he was betraying Jordyn by reporting on her. He hated this situation more with every passing minute. He was to the point where every heartbeat seemed to go in slow motion. He couldn't wait for it to end.

"The gentlemen, and I use the term loosely, stopped by her mailbox before they let themselves into the house. The car they came in dropped them off at the gate and drove away. They got the package and made a phone call. Apparently, somebody didn't like Jordyn's answer. You know the rest. So, I think you're right about her knowing something. I hate to put pressure on you but the sooner we find out what she knows the sooner we can make some arrests and make the world a safer place for her."

"I know," Braeden said. "Can they identify the goon squad?"

"Unfortunately not," Brock responded. "Their night vision camera was malfunctioning. The two agents are going through pictures sent from the LA office right now. Maybe they will come up with something."

"Let me know if they do. It'd be nice to know who to look for."

"We'll do. Take care of yourself, little brother." There was years of love and companionship behind the warmth in the warning.

"Always," Braeden responded.

"This coming from the man who used his body harness as an apparatus to swing him into view of a passing jaguar," Brock said wryly.

"Hey," Braeden said defensively, "that cat was being deliberately obtuse. He didn't want his picture taken."

"The body harness was there for *if* you fell, not *when*."

"So that's what it's for," Braeden said, as if suddenly understanding a great mystery.

He hung up listening to Brock's laugh. When the laughter was gone, Braeden was left alone with his thoughts. He walked into what he now affectionately called the war room. It was where the maps of the farm hung on every available surface. It was where he and Jordyn planned and kept track of camera and trap locations.

He was worried about who the hired goons might be. The level of threat they posed would depend upon whether or not they were hired muscle or if they truly enjoyed terrorizing and/ or killing others.

As his thoughts raced, his eyes traveled around the room. His gaze landed on the topo map that demarked all of his research area. It was speckled with magnetic dots. The red dots showed the live traps. The blue dots showed the Wildlife cams and the yellow dots showed the Nature's View video stations.

His eyes had passed this map several times before it skittered back on the latest pass. He stared at the yellow dots. What if… He ran out the door and up to his apartment. Moments later, he emerged in work clothes, climbed into a buggy, and headed out. He had a blank SD card in one pocket and a 9 millimeter Glock with laser sights in a shoulder holster.

He found what he was looking for. He had set up one of the Nature's View cameras over the spliced fence marking the boundary between Jordyn's property and the National Park. He had taken care to conceal the camera and he was very glad that he had. He smiled grimly as he viewed the footage. It wasn't perfect but it would do. They had seen and avoided two cameras but the lucky number three camera got them. It was set up about twelve feet from the fence crossing. The infrared beam had been tripped by the first goon and caught the second and third man as they jogged behind. Hopefully, the third could be identified by his association with the other two. They had to be headed toward the service road and a waiting car and were probably long gone by now.

Braeden smiled at the baseball bat and pipe carried by Thug Number Two and Thug Number Three respectively. "I wonder what you were doing with those?" He said softly to himself. He quickly changed the SD card and reset the camera.

He climbed back into the buggy and headed homeward. Dawn was creeping into the sky when he finally laid down. The footage was in Brock's inbox. Knowing his conscientious older brother, it would be in the hands of a dozen different experts and the goon squad would be identified before Jordyn made it back to the farm this morning. His last thoughts as he drifted into an exhausted sleep were of Jordyn.

CHAPTER 15

Surprisingly, Jordyn slept through the night. Monica had been unusually quiet even after they made it to the cabin. Jordyn laughed softly to herself at the word cabin. It was more of a log mansion than a cabin. Still, it could have been a noisy hotel room in downtown Pigeon Forge and she would have slept fine. She had been praying silently for help and strength since first pulling up to her house. She kept remembering Pastor Charles's message. She prayed for peace. She had fallen asleep and slept a dreamless, refreshing sleep. She woke feeling that she could face this day. And the next. And the next. Jehovah-jireh.

Jordyn found Monica in one of the massive leather chairs in the living room facing the fireplace. She didn't look like she had slept a wink. She had showered and changed though and made coffee if the wonderful aroma was any indication.

Jordyn sauntered into the room and cheerily said, "Good morn—" Before she finished the greeting, her eyes landed on the shoulder holster she had never seen before. Her eyes flew to Monica's. Monica's eyes were both sad and determined.

"Jordyn, we need to talk." Her tone of voice made Jordyn think that this wouldn't be a particularly pleasant conversation. Jordyn walked to another chair to the left of Monica's and sat down.

"Before, I tell you what I'm about to say, I want you to know that I love you and I never set out to deceive you. I only did what I thought was best." Monica fidgeted a little and added, "I'd hoped you would never find out because I'd hoped you didn't know anything."

She glanced at Jordyn who was waiting expectantly and perplexed by her last statement. "I haven't been entirely honest with you about what I do."

"You mean you're not in charge of security for Wallace Industries?" Jordyn asked, a bit at sea.

"No. I mean, yes. I am in charge of security, but that's not exactly all I do." She took a deep breath and continued. "As you know, Dad dabbles in a bit of everything, import/export, manufacturing, the works. A few years ago, Christy decided to… have a little fun by importing illegally. She started with caviar and Cuban cigars and then into drugs. It was the drugs that got her in trouble."

Monica stood and began pacing in front of the huge rock fireplace with its mantle made out of a huge poplar tree. Perhaps because Jordyn instinctively knew that she really didn't want to hear this that she couldn't help but notice the fireplace and be amazed at the size of the two pillars with half of another making the shelf.

"A representative from the DEA and the FBI came to see me. As the head of security, I was supposed to know what was going on and therefore, their prime suspect. I found out later they knew it was Chris, but they really needed my help. I convinced them to give me twenty-four hours to clear my name and point them in the right direction."

She glanced at Jordyn. "Are you still with me?" At Jordyn's nod she continued, "The trail led to Chris of course, my irresponsible older sister. She confessed all of it. When I told her she could be in serious trouble because the authorities had found out she told me all of the details. She didn't buy much, just a recreational amount as she put it. But Manuel had major shipments coming into the US, which is why what little Chris was doing caught the DEA's attention. Anyway, I went back and told them the story. They believed me. I convinced them that the only way to get Chris' drug supplier, Manuel Velasquez, was if I confronted him as a concerned sister/head of security. They had planned this all along so they went along with *my* plan. In exchange for my help, I asked that no charges be brought against Chris."

Monica paused as she reflected back to that time. She had been scared to death. And exhilarated by the experience of catching the quarry. "It worked. They managed to take him down with enough evidence to put him away for years without a mention of the Wallace name. They were so impressed with my plan that when I mentioned working for them, we worked something out. I continue in my current position, but if something comes up where they need someone like me, I'm available."

Jordyn stared as realization began to dawn. "So, four years ago when you were taking an extended vacation, you were actually—"

"In FBI boot camp." Monica finished for her. "I'm not an actual agent. I'm more of a highly trained asset."

"Does anybody else know about this?" Jordyn asked incredulously.

"Besides my direct superiors, only my Dad knows. We decided not to tell my Mom or any of the rest of my friends and family. I'm useful because I can move in circles that other agents would be spotted in immediately." She gave a small shrug. "If I'm known to work with the FBI, I'm not useful to them."

Jordyn studied Monica's face. She wasn't stupid and she was putting two and two together. "And you're telling me now because of last night, aren't you?"

It was a statement, so Monica didn't pretend to answer it. Pretending between longtime friends such as she and Jordyn was unnecessary.

Monica took a deep, steadying breath. "Jordyn, I need to talk to you about Tommy."

"What about him?" Jordyn asked warily, afraid she knew a portion of the answer. Somehow, she had known something like this would happen when she had found the yearbook and the phone records.

"Did you know Tommy was in the witness protection program?" Monica's question was direct, but not unkindly asked.

The air whooshed out of Jordyn and she sat back in her chair. She shook her head in the negative. She hadn't known, but somehow it all made sense. Now.

"What'd he do?" Jordyn's voice was little more than a whisper.

Monica paused a moment before she began the story. "What Tommy told you about working for Senator Booth of California is true. What he didn't tell you is exactly all that he did for the good senator." She paused again, it wasn't pretty and she hated telling Jordyn about this particular part of Tommy's life. "Along with all of his other duties, he was responsible for getting the senator a continuous supply for his drug habit and aiding his penchant for expensive prostitutes. This part of his job entailed dealing with some pretty rough characters. What neither Tommy nor the senator counted on was that the suppliers were under FBI and DEA surveillance."

Monica again began to pace. She was more nervous about Tommy's story than she had been her own. No, that wasn't true. She was more nervous about Jordyn's reaction to it.

"We were about to approach Tommy and the senator to work out a deal of no jail time in exchange for their testimony against the Asian gangsters who supplied the drugs and their businessman boss when Senator Booth killed one of the ladies of the evening."

Jordyn held her breath, waiting to hear what Tommy had done.

"Tommy told the panicked senator to take care of his own dirty work and quit. The senator threatened Tommy's life so he ran. He cleaned out all the incriminating evidence he had, including conversations he recorded for his own protection, and ran with it. Two days later, he contacted the FBI, said his conscience wouldn't allow him to keep quiet about the girl."

Jordyn felt a flood of relief. His morality was skewed. Drugs and prostitution were okay and murder was not, but at least he'd tried to make it right in the end. Still, she couldn't help but wonder if she had known him at all. She couldn't reconcile the man she had loved and married with the kind of man who would facilitate such behavior.

Monica continued after taking a drink of her barely warm coffee. "He gave us a mountain of evidence against both the senator and the suppliers, but he held back evidence of a criminal connection to Henry Lee, the drug ring financer. That's why I was in the case. Mr. Lee owns an import/export business and moves in some of the same circles as Wallace Industries. I was his date to a few gatherings, but couldn't prove his connection. Anyway, we knew Mr. Lee was involved but had only circumstantial evidence. Tommy had a card sent from Mr. Lee to the senator. The card refers to the senator's taste in candy and that Mr. Lee and his associates enjoy doing business with a US senator. It also mentions how refreshing it was to find that political corruption was as rampant in the US as it was in China."

Jordyn asked, "Tommy still had the card when he died?" At Monica's nod she asked, "Why did he feel he needed to keep it?"

"Tommy correctly believed that Mr. Lee was the biggest threat to his life. Tommy used the card for protection. As long as he was alive, Mr. Lee's card was safe."

"So, Tommy's death wasn't an accident?" Jordyn had suspected this when she found out about the calls to Tommy's cell phone. But Monica's affirmative nod caused a wave of fresh grief to break over her as unrelenting as icy ocean waves. Did he know he was going to die in his final minutes?

"Against the advice of his handler, Tommy left the program when he decided to marry you. That left him vulnerable if he was found. We're pretty sure that the implicated suppliers and the senator are responsible for it. What they didn't know was that Tommy had already taped his testimony. His death only makes them look guiltier."

Monica sat down and waited for Jordyn to get angry, cry, or scream at her. Jordyn's still face worried her more than hysterics. Her calm was unnatural.

"How did Tommy get the name Grey?" When he'd introduced himself as Tommy Grey in New York City, Jordyn had thought he was kidding. It had always seemed odd.

Jordyn's question surprised Monica. "I had been used in the case a couple of times as Lee's date and as an agent on the ground at invitation only political parties. I knew Tommy would need every advantage he could so I suggested the name to Br… Tommy's handler in the US Marshal's Service." She laughed a little. "I picked a name that reminded me of honesty, trust, and integrity. Everything your family stands for and everything I thought Tommy lacked. Imagine my surprise and dismay when you met him in a café in Manhatten." She hoped Jordyn hadn't heard the slip. Braeden had the right to tell his own story.

"So, what does all of this have to do with last night?"

"Mr. Lee has evidently decided to retrieve the card."

"But I don't know anything about the card." Jordyn protested.

"Are you sure, Jordyn?" Monica's question made Jordyn glare at her. "I'm sorry but I know the demolition squad took whatever Braeden put in your mailbox last night." She inwardly cringed at the betrayal in Jordyn's eyes.

Jordyn decided to come clean. Monica probably knew it anyway if her phone was tapped.

As if reading her thoughts Monica said, "Your phone's not tapped if that's what you think, but your house is under constant surveillance."

Jordyn nodded and then started talking. She told Monica about everything leading up to the phone call. "I got a call Monday evening and they gave me instructions to leave the paper in the box and then leave the farm." She shrugged helplessly. "I didn't know what they wanted so I went looking. I found where I thought they must have called Tommy on our old cell phone records. I made a copy and left it in the mailbox, asking what exactly they wanted." She managed a small smile. "I guess I know now."

"I'm sure they didn't want to tell you what they were looking for or why. It would be one more person who knew of Mr. Lee's less than legitimate connections."

Jordyn suddenly stood. "Well, I'm going to get some coffee before I head home. Do you want another cup?"

Monica stared at her incredulously. "You can't be serious! Haven't you been listening? Tommy was in the witness protection program," She said it slowly, as if that would help Jordyn understand. "They don't put you in there because it's fun for people to disappear. It's too dangerous for you to go home as if nothing has happened."

Jordyn gave Monica a steady look. "I don't intend to act like nothing happened. Apparently, I've had the FBI, the US Marshal's Service, and who knows who else watching me. It's possible that they are satisfied that I don't know anything. I think the weirdness of last night was to scare me just in case I did know something." She talked over top of Monica's protestations. "Anyway, we're not going to find the card with me hiding out somewhere. No one knew Tommy's quirks better than me. You may have known his history better, but not his everyday routine. You and your FBI compadres can stay at the farm and search to your heart's content if that'll make you feel better, but I'm going home."

Monica nodded, accepting her inevitable defeat in this argument. She reached for her ringing cell phone as Jordyn headed to the kitchen.

"How'd it go?" Luke's voice was as testy as ever.

"Good morning to you too, Luke," Monica deliberately added an extra dose of cheery sarcasm.

"Monica, I told you good morning when you called me at 3:00 a.m. to tell me that you were going to add to your list of sins by telling Jordyn all about the FBI's secret weapon against the higher classes." His sarcasm wasn't appreciated. "Now, I want to know how it went. Did she tell you anything?" It didn't seem that Luke had gotten much sleep either.

"It went better than expected. She took it in stride. She doesn't know where the card is, but we've been invited to look anywhere we like."

"Really," Luke sounded happier at the thought of doing something besides watching Jordyn chase critters around and have dinner at fancy restaurants. "I'll have a team there in an hour. You need to make contact with Brock Parker about Jordyn's safe house. His number—"

"I have his number and she's not going." Monica interrupted his rapid words.

"What!" Luke bellowed.

"You don't have to shout, Luke. I can hear just fine. At least, I could before you yelled in my ear. She says she's going home and that we can occupy the bunkhouse if we feel the need, but she won't leave."

"That's ludicrous!"

"I know."

"She could get killed."

"She knows that and thinks it unlikely."

"Well, it's nice to know that there are suddenly so many experts in unexpected places." He paused and sighed heavily. "Can't you talk her into going away for a week or so at least?"

Monica laughed and since she didn't appreciate vindictiveness she said, "I would have about as much chance of doing that as you do of getting a promotion off of this case."

Luke's answer was a disconnected call. Monica was guessing that he would be needing a new cell phone. Oh well, at least he wasn't insisting that they kidnap Jordyn and take her to a safe house. And it was so fun making him mad.

Jordyn appeared a moment later, bag in one hand and mug in the other. "Let's roll."

CHAPTER 16

By 9:00 p.m. that night, the house looked immaculate. Pastor Charles's grandson was one of the first responding officers to the scene. He had called Ann and mentioned that they might want to stop by and check on Jordyn. They had and found Braeden cleaning a section of the living room before heading out to check his traps. Within an hour, over half of the congregation was there, cleaning up glass and busted furniture and replacing scattered items. All in all, they were even having a good time. Furniture was brought to replace the battered couches and chairs. The talented photographer at Walls Photography Studio took the portrait of Jordyn's father and some of the other frames in for repair. Mr. Phillips, the local antique dealer, promised to take her grandfather's desk in for repairs that would make it "as good as new."

Jordyn couldn't believe the outpouring of love. Ann smiled. "We're all part of the family of God and we share our sorrow as well as our joy."

As the afternoon passed into the evening, over one hundred people had stopped by to help, haul off discarded items, or deliver new ones. Jordyn had ordered food from Mom and Pop's for lunch and dinner was brought from The Pizza Place. The church folks just assumed the FBI were more of Jordyn's friends that had come to help. No one even mentioned that they only looked through papers. Luke walked around checking the security system claiming to be a security specialist. Monica kept following Jordyn around a bit like a faithful puppy. Add the alarm going off occasionally as the "expert" tried to determine exactly how it was bypassed and there was glorious chaos.

Throughout the day, Tommy was never far from Jordyn's mind. It felt odd considering that Braeden had been so much in her thoughts lately. This morning, he'd worked for a while and then set off to check traps. He'd told her he was leaving and waved on his way out the door, but they had very little contact all day. Still, she had questions about Tommy and she wanted the answer to one right now. She turned to find Monica where she had been most of the day, right behind her. "Mon, how long was Tommy in the program?"

Monica saw no reason to hide it now. "About a year."

Tommy had told Jordyn when they met that he was between jobs due to a major career change and that he was looking into being a circus performer. Jordyn couldn't help but smile at the memory. For proof of his ability to be a circus perfomer Tommy had picked up three apples from a basket on the café counter and juggled them for her. It was a memorable first meeting.

Even though she didn't understand the smile, Monica was surprised to see it instead of tears. Jordyn seemed so at peace. Maybe it was the God thing that Jordyn was involved in. She hoped it lasted through the next secret.

After promising to host the church picnic at summer's end, Jordyn waved away the last of the helpers, Pastor Charles and Ann. They were the first to come and the last to leave. Jordyn knew that the magnitude of help was because of the love and respect given to the couple by their congregation. She recalled telling the pastor how much she found herself relying on his words from

Sunday morning. "I appreciate you being God's mouthpiece to me. I don't think anyone could have said it better."

He had humbly bowed his head and said, "You're kind to an old man."

As she watched them disappear down her tree-lined drive, she drew comfort from knowing that she was in their constant prayers.

Monica sat in the kitchen watching Braeden heat a pan of tomato pizza. The three of them hadn't eaten supper and he wanted to keep busy. He was restlessly pulling the dish towel through the loose fist of one hand. While Jordyn was seeing her pastor and his wife to the door, Monica decided to put him out of his misery.

"I didn't tell Jordyn that you're working with the US Marshal's Service, but I think you should."

Braeden almost jumped at the sound of her voice he was so tense. He gave her a grateful look. "I didn't know for sure if you knew."

Monica shrugged. "Luke told me today but I had already figured it out. It helped immensely to know your brother. I met Brock in Los Angeles when I was working on the Lee case. He has a picture of the three of you on a fishing trip. I remembered when my boss told me that the US Marshal's Service had someone undercover and you just happened to be the only new person in Jordyn's otherwise lonely life."

Braeden nodded. He considered her advice as he pulled the bubbling pizza out of the oven. He was relieved at discovering Jordyn didn't yet know of his full role in her life. He'd wanted to talk to her all day but between the cleanup and checking the traps, he hadn't had a chance. On the last trip out, he'd decided that he was going to talk to her tonight.

"You genuinely care for her don't you?" Monica sounded surprised.

"Yes," Braeden said simply.

"It's easy to love Jordyn."

"I know." The simple statement spoke volumes.

"Try not to hurt her." Monica leaned toward him slightly. "If you want advice from someone who's known Jordyn for a very long time and has been in your shoes, just tell her the truth."

"I plan to. And I don't plan to hurt either of us." Braeden's response was what Monica wanted to hear.

She leaned back and they smiled at each other in mutual understanding. Jordyn picked that moment to stroll into the kitchen. "It's nice to see such harmony between one's friends. What's so funny?" She asked innocently.

Monica was thinking how nice it was to see Jordyn sending a special smile toward Braeden. She hoped she still felt the same after he told her his secret.

Braeden was thinking how wonderful it was to be close to Jordyn. He smiled at her as he walked toward her and pulled her into a close hug.

Monica stood. "Well, I can see I'm no longer needed in the kitchen area. I'll be checking out your new couch and wolf documentary while eating my pizza." She wasn't sure anybody heard her.

Braeden couldn't believe how much he'd missed Jordyn. They'd spent almost every day together since April. It was now July and he couldn't believe how important she had become to him in so short a time.

He pulled back slightly and looked into her beautiful eyes. "Hey, you."

Jordyn smiled up at Braeden and couldn't help feeling content. Oddly enough, finding out all of the things about Tommy that she hadn't known didn't put a damper on her feelings for Braeden. If anything, the new found knowledge had given her a measure of closure. Her marriage and Tommy's actions made sense now. She knew their relationship still wasn't on a par with what she had wanted, but it wasn't a complete disaster as she had thought for so long.

"Hey to you too," she said softly and kissed his chin.

"That'll get you into trouble." Braeden teased gently.

Jordyn cocked her head in the characteristically familiar gesture. "How much trouble?"

"It might get you a kiss." He grinned mischievously.

Jordyn smiled slyly and aimed for his chin again. He intercepted with his lips and gave her a long, soft kiss. He tried to put everything he was feeling into that kiss. He tried to show her how much he loved her with the intimacy of that special touch. He pulled back and looked into her eyes. "How're you holding up?"

Jordyn reflected on that question. "I've found out a lot over the last twenty-four hours that would have devastated me a few months ago. But somehow, I feel at peace. I feel asleep praying last night and I can't shake the feeling that everything is going to work out."

"Monica told me a bit about Tommy earlier today and that she had a secret she felt you should know as well." He looked directly into her eyes and wondered how he could ever risk telling her his own secret. "Are you sure you're okay?"

Jordyn gave him a tight squeeze. "I'm tired and feel like I have dealt with a mountain of emotional secrets today, but I'm fine."

Braeden smiled and asked, "Are you hungry? I've heated some pizza."

"Sounds marvelous. I'll be back as soon as I wash my hands."

Braeden put the cooling pizza onto two plates and filled two glasses with soda. He'd felt that you should always drink soda with pizza since he was a child and his parents had only allowed him and his hyper siblings to drink it on pizza night.

He was honestly trying to plan how to tell her who he was when she came back into the room. She was smiling at him so sweetly and her face looked so tired that he decided to wait until tomorrow. She had dealt with way too much in the past few days. Braeden, Jordyn, and Monica fell asleep watching the wolves overcome the hardship of the winter, awakening when the credits were rolling. Braeden headed out to his apartment after making internal excuses for not talking to Jordyn. He was calling himself a fool and a coward as he climbed into bed and turned out his light.

CHAPTER 17

The day after the big cleanup, Faith arrived for their belated lunch date. The three friends laughed and talked all through the lunch of scrumptious sandwiches made by none other than Luke Stettleman. Surprisingly, Monica didn't tease him about the food. She said a quiet thanks as she carried them out to the kitchen patio where Faith was hearing the details of the damaged house from Jordyn. She already knew of Monica's role due to a *long* conversation the two had the day before when Monica called to cancel the lunch date.

"I think your church's response was great. That's how Christians should be with each other." She scrunched her face at Monica and Jordyn. "I still wish that I could've helped though."

"Your mom said you were sick and that was that," Jordyn said laughingly. It was a long-standing joke that Faith's mom was overprotective of her daughter.

Monica chimed in. "And the fewer people who know about my extracircular activities, the safer I am. Furthermore, Jordyn wouldn't even let me tell her family so if you came to help, we would have had even more explanations to make."

"I'll tell them when it's over, which will hopefully be soon." Jordyn took a sip of her lemonade and added, "They identified the three stooges who rearranged the house and picked them up at the airport in Knoxville. Also, there's another witness willing to link Henry Lee with the suppliers and it's not a far stretch to the senator after that. Apparently, they've all got more important things to worry about than little 'ol me."

Faith shook her head. "Are you sure you have no idea where else to look for the card?"

"None. I'm sure Tommy had it but for all I know he got rid of it before the crash."

Faith and Monica were quiet as Jordyn appeared lost in thought. Finally, Jordyn began to talk. "I need to tell you guys what I wanted to tell you at our ill-fated lunch Wednesday."

She told them about her wonderful courtship and the contradictory tumultuousness of her marriage. They listened with interest and attention. She told them the same story she had told Braeden not long after he'd arrived. They all cried and when it was over, Jordyn was glad she had finally told them the whole truth.

"After thinking, we had a much poorer relationship than I had believed, I find out that he was just trying to protect me. Even though I wish he'd just been honest in the beginning, I'm more content with our short life together now. Still, I regret the turmoil of our last weeks."

"He was just trying to protect you much the same as I did." Monica interjected.

"Honesty is always the best policy though." Jordyn insisted as she set her glass of lemonade back on the table.

She looked up to see Braeden standing at the top of the patio steps. She thought he looked a little pale. Only Monica knew why.

"Hey, do you want a sandwich? They're really good." Jordyn offered.

"No, I was just going to let you know that I'm going on the camera run and that I probably won't make it back for supper because I'm going to check the traps as soon as the cameras are all checked."

"Okay. Be careful."

Jordyn thought he acted a little odd but wrote it off as his desire not to interfere in an all-girl lunch. She would have to tell him she didn't care if he had a sandwich with them. They were done with the serious stuff anyway.

She didn't get a chance to talk to him though because he didn't make it back before dark and uncharacteristically went straight to his apartment.

A day later, Jordyn stared intently at Braeden. He was aiming the dart gun at the wolf's hip. He gently squeezed the trigger. A few minutes later, they were working quickly to collect data and tag the wolf. Braeden was thrilled to discover that it was a healthy four-year-old female. She didn't have a tag but she had had a litter of spring pups.

"She's beautiful," Jordyn said in awe as Braeden released her leg from the trap and gently checked it.

"It's awesome to be this close. It never ceases to amaze me," Braeden said in a half whisper.

They collected blood and hair samples. They weighed her and aged her. Braeden gave her several vaccinations and let Jordyn rub the area distended by the medicine under her skin in order to disperse it, while he gave her a quick but thorough physical exam.

"She's as good as they come," Braeden said happily. "Maybe we will find her litter sometime."

They finished in record time and Braeden placed the wolf on the trail and headed back down the path toward the road where they'd left the buggy. They found a place with some good cover and waited as the wolf woke up. She worked herself to her feet and headed off the trail to a small stream. She drank thirstily before heading out on her way with hardly a wobble.

Jordyn grinned into Braeden's beaming face. "This is amazing and the most fun I've ever had. I can't believe you get paid to do this." She jabbed him playfully in the ribs.

Braeden gave her a smug, self-satisfied smirk. "It's even better than owning your own amusement park."

Jordyn shrugged. "I would probably agree but I can't remember the park very much because Granddad closed it before my time."

Braeden almost ran off of the road as he stared at Jordyn. "You're kidding!"

Jordyn grinned. "Nope. We can still go to Dollywood though if you would like to go."

Braeden shook his head and laughed. He'd been kidding but trust Jordyn to have trumped him.

The next day they went to Dollywood after Braeden had checked the traps earlier that morning. Jordyn was like a small child as she went from one ride to the next. It was nice to have a day to play and try and forget the dark cloud hanging over them at present. When they entered the park, she got a map and solemnly informed him the best route through the park. "We always go up the left toward Thunderhead, Timber Canyon, and Mystery Mine then back past Tennessee Tornado, Blazing Fury, Daredevil Falls and into the Country Fair."

Braeden cocked an eyebrow. "We have to do it this way, huh?"

Jordyn nodded seriously. "Otherwise, you get sidetracked on the way in and you don't get to finish riding everything."

Braeden laughed and took her hand as they headed up the hill toward their first ride. After riding Thunderhead three times, they moved on throughout the park. They rode a ton of rides and looked through as many shops before Braeden declared the need to sit. So, they watched the captive eagle show, ate lunch at the Ranger's Cookhouse, and rode the Ferris Wheel. Braeden enjoyed the Ferris Wheel because he stole a kiss every time they made it to the top, although the train ride with Jordyn snuggled tightly against him was really nice too.

The shops were truly amazing. Braeden had never seen anything like what the artisans there produced. Jordyn bought him a letter opener with a wolf carved into the end from one of the many shops. He won a huge bear for Jordyn with a water pistol and presented it to her with a wide grin. He was surprised at how proud he was to have won it on his first try.

Jordyn took the offered bear and squeezed it in a tight hug. "Thanks, Braeden." She didn't tell him that the bear was as special to her as a piece of expensive jewelry. The look of pride on his face at being able to hand his girl the bear was priceless and the bear would always remind her of it.

After snapping a picture of Braeden watching the eagle show, a park employee offered to take their picture together. Just as he was about to snap the shot, Braeden's hand found the ticklish spot on Jordyn's side. Instead of a smiling couple facing the camera, the picture captured Jordyn and Braeden looking into one another's eyes, laughing at the joy of life and love.

After the Tennessee Twister, Jordyn insisted on getting a refreshing dessert at the Berries and Cream stand.

"Aren't you going to let your stomach settle after that ride?" a queasy Braeden asked.

"On no, I'm fine." Jordyn said with one of her fabulous smiles. "Besides, eating berries and cream is part of the atmosphere," she said as she waved her hands in the air to indicate the park at large.

"That's what you said about the frozen lemonade," Braeden replied.

"And I was right too, wasn't I?" Jordyn pointed out triumphantly.

Braeden shook his head in acquiescence. As they headed to the stand promising cold goodness in a spoon Braeden asked, "So what else do we just *have* to do as part of the whole experience?"

Braeden didn't understand Jordyn's grin until later when he found himself running through spouts of water in Dreamland

Forest, trying to catch her. The expressions on the faces of the small kids watching them clearly indicated that they thought the grownups who had invaded their water playground were acting very silly. Braeden could have told them that some day, they would love someone to the point that silly was redefined.

Jordyn fell asleep on the way home and after he dropped her off, Braeden headed out to check the traps before dark. He didn't even try to dodge the fact that he was making excuses for not telling her the truth. He just wanted a few more days with her before he possibly ruined their relationship.

CHAPTER 18

The next day they did find the litter of pups—three males and five females. They took an inordinate amount of time to tag them, partly due to handling them with latex gloves to keep the human scent down and partly because his assistant was more interested in playing with the pups than checking and tagging them. She found that they liked the strings dangling from her shirt and that was the end of her help. When he asked her to help and stop acting like she was trying to pick one to take home, she almost looked hopeful. Braeden's sharp, "Don't even think about it!" caused her to shrug and finally help him give the pups their vaccinations.

By keeping an eye on the den and setting traps on the trails nearby, they were able to tag the whole pack and retag two of the wolves that had been released two years ago. It was a small triumph to see them healthy and settled. Braeden was glad that he and Jordyn had been able to tag and vaccinate the whole pack. He was pleased with their population growth and suspected that even more wolves were roaming the national park that was adjacent to Jordyn's west boundary.

As they worked in the field, it was easy to forget the FBI standing guard at the house. Braeden was reminded of the situation and his part in it every evening when they came dragging in, tired but happy. He kept putting off talking to Jordyn about the fact that he had come here not only to study the wolves but her as well. Monica kept telling him to "Tell her already!" And unfortunately for Braeden, he kept finding excuses not to.

The case was going well. The prosecuting attorney felt that they wouldn't need the card to cinch the case, but the FBI decided to hang around until after all of the arrests had been made. It was going to be a huge bust. They needed to arrest everyone involved as simultaneously as possible so no one would have the chance to slip away.

CHAPTER 19

Jordyn found herself smiling happily as her father, Patrick Grey, talked to Braeden about red wolves. Her mother and father had surprised her at lunch with a visit and they had all decided to spend the day together. Jordyn had told them about her marriage, the phone calls, and the case. Her mother cried when Jordyn told them about Tommy.

"I'm so sorry about Tommy, Jordyn," her mother said as she squeezed her baby's hand.

"It's not your fault." Jordyn sighed. "To be honest, I'm glad the truth came out. I don't think I could have moved on with my life until I had closure over my relationship with Tommy."

"And do you think Braeden Parker has a place in your new life?"

Jordyn brought startled eyes to her father. "How did you know about Braeden?"

Both of her parents laughed. "I noticed weeks ago that something might be brewing between you two. Now that we're here, it's plain that you care a great deal for him, sweetheart," her mother responded.

Jordyn couldn't help the smile as she thought about Braeden. "That's not quite true, Mom."

At her mother's surprised look, Jordyn laughed and shrugged. "I love him." The wonder in her voice wasn't lost on either parent. "I love him more than I ever thought it possible to love another human being." The confession to her parents made Jordyn happier than she had been in a long time. Except when she was with Braeden.

Her mother's tear-filled eyes told her how glad she was to hear it. Her father cleared his throat and asked, "So glad to meet the man you who stole your heart."

Later that evening, Jordyn was sitting on one of her new couches, snuggled up to Braeden's side. He'd slipped an arm behind her and laid it on the back of the couch. It ended up resting on Jordyn and she had reached up to grasp the hand hanging over her shoulder. He sent her a special smile before going back to his conversation with her father. She met Dinah Grey's eyes and they shared a smile that only women who have loved deeply can understand.

Braeden was profoundly happy. That's the only way he could describe it. Jordyn snuggled up to his side just felt right. Her hand fit his perfectly. He gave it another squeeze as he sat talking to Patrick Grey, enjoying the slender strength and smoothness of her hand in his. Life was good. And hopefully, it would only get better. He was going to talk to Jordyn the day he found out her parents were coming so he had to put his tale on hold for now. As soon as they left, he was going to tell her everything, including the fact that he loved her.

Days later, after the Parkers had decided to spend the week, Braeden couldn't believe how nervous he was. The Parkers had been there for three days and he found that he liked them both a great deal. As the week went by, his respect for the family grew.

They were not only good people, but they were Godly people. He had spoken often with Patrick Grey on a variety of subjects and he was impressed by how wise the man was, not only on business matters but on the Bible. His newfound discovery of how wonderful the family was didn't calm his stomach though. He was still extremely nervous. But in all fairness, he had never asked for a woman's hand in marriage before.

He was nodding absently at something the older man had said when Patrick stopped and looked at him. "Son, I believe in being honest and forthright. You've clearly got something you want to say and I think you should say it before you choke on it."

Braeden gave him a grateful smile. "I know you haven't known me very long and that this may come as a surprise." Braeden paused before he blurted out. "Sir, I want to marry your daughter."

To Braeden's surprise, Patrick chuckled. "I can't say that it's a shock."

"Sir?" Braeden hadn't realized that they had seen them as anything more than a dating couple. Apparently, they had seen in them the same thing Braeden had, a perfect match.

"Dinah and I have been watching you two since we arrived. You have something special." He paused. "Have you asked Jordyn yet?"

"No, sir. I wanted to ask you first."

Patrick nodded, impressed and pleased with the respect he was being shown. "Son, I would be proud for her to marry you, but the decision is hers. Although I don't think I could stop her." At Braeden's panicked look he quickly added, "And I wouldn't try."

He turned and continued walking toward the porch. "I think you're a good man, Braeden. I think you love my daughter. However, I can't get past the feeling that you're hiding something." Braeden was trying to think of a response when Patrick sat down on the top step of the porch and indicated to Braeden to do the same. "In a world fraught with secrets of late, I don't think that's a good thing. Jordyn's happiness is important to me. I think Tommy made her happy for a time. But I have to admit, there's more to it than that. Jordyn needs a man who will let her be who she is. She didn't get that chance with Tommy."

At Braeden's nod, Patrick continued, "When Jordyn was about fourteen, Dinah and I decided to teach our children the value of money. We hadn't spoiled them as much as we could have, but we felt that they needed to learn how to do without. We cut them back to what we considered a normal allowance of five dollars per week." He chuckled as he thought back. "There was a whole lot of moaning at first. The boys were at dating age and they had to get very inventive to get the girls to go on a picnic instead of to a fancy restaurant. About three weeks into it, Jordyn came to me and asked for at least five hundred dollars and told me she might need more. I was getting ready to tell her no when I remembered that Jordyn hadn't complained when we changed their allowance. In fact, I couldn't recall when she had ever really asked for anything that expensive before." He smiled fondly as he continued, "When I asked her what she needed it for, she took me to the barn. There on the floor was a very sick Doberman. She was in obviously poor health and had been grossly neglected. When Jordyn walked to her, that pitiful dog lifted her head and licked her hand. She acted as though Jordyn was the best thing that had ever happened to her." He glanced at Braeden to see if he was following. "She had a lump behind her left shoulder and Jordyn wanted to take her to the vet." He shrugged. "I gave her the money." Tears filled his eyes as Patrick recounted the story, "She nursed that old dog back to health. It became a much loved family pet. I noticed a change in Jordyn after that. She started taking an interest in the Grey Foundation. She had never been callous, but she was so giving afterward that in comparison she almost seemed to have been callous toward others. A few months later, I asked Jordyn why she was so set on helping that dog. I wanted to know what my fourteen year-old daughter had seen that I couldn't." He stopped and looked Braeden in the eye. "She told me that when the dog wandered into the yard, she expected her to shy away because of a lack of positive human interaction. But instead, she looked at Jordyn with hope in her big, brown canine eyes. What grabbed Jordyn was that the dog *could* hope even after years of abuse and neglect. I think she gave a bit of that hope to Jordyn because I saw a big change in Jordyn after that. Her eyes seemed to sparkle with hope—the hope of love, happiness, and goodness in life." He sighed. "I was afraid that I would never see that again because it's been gone since Tommy's death." He met Braeden's eyes. "Until this past week." He stood and Braeden rose to stand beside of him. He turned and looked at Braeden with eyes that seemed to see through him, a father's eyes. "She's had more than enough secrets and heartache in her life. I didn't think she would bounce back after…" His voice trailed off. After a moment he quietly said, "Please don't take my little girl's hope away."

Braeden nodded and stood still as Patrick went in the front door. The Grey's were leaving this evening and he would talk to Jordyn first thing in the morning. Braeden had struggled over talking to her long enough and he had finally decided to do what felt right. He had a secret to tell her. And hopefully, a question to ask.

CHAPTER 20

Jordyn swam vigorously before finally flipping to her back and floating around the pool. It was almost 12:30 at night. Her mom and dad had left early that evening, and she and Braeden had cooked dinner together. They had a wonderful time. She had felt so close to Braeden, like she had known him forever. But for some reason, the look in Braeden's eyes when he'd left disturbed her to the point that she couldn't sleep. He'd had a look filled with the oddest mix of both doubt and…hope. After trying to fall asleep for an hour, she had decided on a swim and was glad that she had. When she felt that she could finally go to sleep, she headed toward the door leading to the kitchen patio.

Rather than drip water all through her house, she changed her mind and decided to slip into her robe in the large changing room at the end of the building. She walked to the other end of the pool and stepped into the room. She was about to change when her eyes lit on the wall of eight lockers that Tommy had wanted installed. Without really thinking about it, Jordyn headed to the locker that Tommy had used. She had never cleaned it out and quick tears filled her eyes when she saw a pair of navy swimming trunks with a white stripe down the side hanging ready for use. Ear plugs were lying haphazardly where he'd left them. She reached for them and carefully placed them back in their container. She was about to close the locker door when she noticed a glint of silver in the back of the container. She pushed the trunks to the side and looked in. Sure enough, there was a small door protected with a combination padlock.

Jordyn chewed on her lip. She didn't have the combination and she didn't know if she wanted to open it anyway. In all honesty, she didn't know if she wanted to deal with something Tommy felt he should hide. On the other hand, the card might be in the locker. She decided she would try a few obvious combinations and if that didn't work, she would get Braeden to look at it tomorrow.

She flipped the dial to the digits of Tommy's birthday, her birthday, their anniversary and nothing happened. She was about to give up when she remembered something from their honeymoon. Their cottage number had been 7342. After a wonderful day on the beach together, swimming, sailing, parasailing, and enjoying the comforts of a private island, they had walked to their cottage in the evening light. Tommy declared that everything about the island was perfect as he'd twirled her in the air. He'd laughed as he said whimsically that even their cottage number was perfect. She flipped the dial again. It opened. Somehow, Jordyn knew what she would find before she even looked. A white envelope held a white card. The envelope was addressed to Senator Booth. So, he'd had it all along. She would call Monica tomorrow and get it into the right hands.

She was about to slide it back into the safe when she saw another envelope. Her name was scrawled across the front in Tommy's familiar hand. Almost in a dreamlike state she pulled the sheets out of the envelope and read.

Dear Jordyn,

You probably know of my faults and failures by now or you wouldn't be reading this. I put the safe in myself the day after we got back from our honeymoon, and I'm sure you know why I did. You have no idea how often I've wrestled with telling you everything, especially now. Every day I wake up and see the pain in your eyes and I hate myself for getting you involved in my troubles. I was selfish and now you are paying the price. I want you to know that none of this is your fault. Stop shaking your head. It's not your fault. I know you. You've probably been blaming yourself and considered our arguments your responsibility somehow. They're not. The blame lies with me. I know this and I don't want our marriage to fall apart because of my stupid mistakes, so I'm going to meet with the Senator in an hour. Hopefully, after today I won't worry to the point of picking a fight every time you get behind the wheel and head out shopping, to church, or out with friends. I thought I could keep the situation under control, but I can't. I recorded the conversation arranging our meeting. It's in the home movies marked Tommy's Niagara Jump. I know, it's a corny name, but I thought you might get a kick out of it. If anything happens, I'm sure someone will be by for it. Just look for the guys in the dark, boring suits.

I've thought a lot about what I would like my last words to you to be. I still don't know exactly what to say. I would like to put everything I feel for you into words and I know that words just aren't adequate enough. I would like to tell you how sorry I am that I've hurt you. I would like to tell you how much meaning my life has since I've been with you. I would like you to know that I love you more than I ever thought it was possible to love another. For the first time in my life, I love someone more than myself. I know our life together hasn't been the bliss you deserve, but I wouldn't trade a minute of being with you for all of the safety in the world for me. You've made me the happiest I've ever been. I need you to believe that. Not only have you loved me, but you've pointed me to God's love. Sounds crazy coming from me, doesn't it? But it's true. This morning, when I decided to talk to the Senator, I knew I needed more than any earthly protection. Oddly enough, I feel at peace about it all. God is good, but I wouldn't have come to that conclusion without you pointing the way. So, thank you.

I've told you I love you and I've thanked you for pointing me to my Savior. What I'm going to say next hurts like crazy but I'm going to say it because it's the best thing for you. Jordyn, if something happens to me I want you to give love another chance. Please don't live your life alone. You have a lot of love to give. You have been a wonderful wife to me and I know you will be a great mother. Don't throw that away because your first husband wasn't what he should be. But if you do not believe anything I have told you, (and I wouldn't blame you if you don't trust me anymore) believe that I love you. I love you more than you could ever know. Please don't hate me.

Tommy

It took Jordyn several minutes to realize that she was crumpled onto the floor of the changing room, tears dripping from her face onto the white pages, smearing the long dried black ink. He'd loved her. She knew that with a certainty. He had loved her and he had found the Lord. Her tears were tears of both joy and sorrow. She was glad he'd finally gone to the Lord for help. The sorrow over what she would like to tell him was vying with her joy. He hadn't been a bad husband. He'd been scared. She had loved him. A part of her loved him still. She wanted to tell him that and cried because she couldn't. She remembered how people said that you always want one more day with a loved one to tell them all of the things you wished you'd said while they were alive.

Later, as she lay in bed and was drifting off to sleep, she felt grateful that Tommy had written to her. "A part of me will always love you, Tommy." A tear slid down her cheek as she said all of the things she wanted to tell him. "I think we would have grown old together if time had allowed us to. Thank you for loving me and giving me the freedom to love again." The last words were said only in her mind as she drifted into sleep.

CHAPTER 21

Braeden never could figure out what woke him up, but at 3:00 a.m. he found himself heading toward the kitchen for something to drink. He passed by his cell phone and out of habit picked it up. He was shocked to find seven missed calls. Alarm slammed through him as he saw Brock's name as the one responsible for all of the missed calls. He quickly pressed send and headed to get his pants and shoes.

Brock didn't take the time for niceties. "Braeden, the witness in the Lee case was killed about an hour ago. That puts Jordyn right in the bull's eye."

"How close is the FBI?" Braeden was fighting down the panic.

"ETA is fifteen minutes. Can you get to Jordyn?" Brock knew the risk he was putting his brother in and he hated it.

"I've got to call Jordyn," was Braeden's only response before the call was ended.

Braeden was already heading down the steps with gun drawn when Jordyn answered the phone. He could tell that he had clearly woke her out of a deep sleep. "Jordyn, I need you to let me in."

"Braeden, what's the matter?" Her voice sounded a bit disoriented.

"Jordyn, I don't have time to explain. I really need you to open the door now." The urgency in his voice had her waiting at the open door before he got there. Braeden shoved her inside and locked the door behind him.

"Braeden, what is the matter?" Jordyn's voice was laced with fear at his manner and the gun.

"The witness in the Lee case was killed." As realization dawned in her face and fear built he added, "The FBI are on the way."

He hustled her down the hall and into her room. When she reached for the hall light he stopped her. "Don't. If someone's out there, we don't want them to think we know something's up."

She looked at him questioningly and then at the gun. He groaned inwardly. He should have talked to her before now. "Get some clothes on," he said.

"Where are we going to go?" Jordyn's question was a good one and he didn't really have an answer for it.

"I'm not sure but I don't want to be where they know you are."

Without another word, Jordyn grabbed some clothes and headed toward the bathroom. Braeden waited impatiently for her to change. Each second felt like an eternity. His adrenaline was pumping and he felt like he would explode if he waited any longer. Just as he turned toward the bathroom to snap at Jordyn to hurry, he sensed rather than heard a stirring at the door. He stepped to the side of the door just as Jordyn came out of the bathroom. The man entering the room never knew what hit him as Braeden brought his gun butt down on the man's skull. He fell to the floor and didn't move.

Braeden found Jordyn's hand and gestured for her to be quiet. She met his eyes in alarm when they heard stirrings from the long hallway. Obviously, whoever was out there had heard their cohort's heavy fall and was proceeding with caution. No longer concerned about the noise, Braeden grabbed the French door leading from Jordyn's room to the porch and threw it open.

With Jordyn in one hand and his gun in the other he ran toward the barn. He heard a shout behind them and zigzagged just in time to hear a sound whip past his ear. They had silencers.

They ran into the barn, but rather than stop and hide they ran to the back door and into the field beyond, effectively putting the barn between them and the house. "Shouldn't we try to hide in the barn until help comes?" Jordyn asked.

Braeden shook his head and kept moving forward in a low crouch. "That's what they will expect us to do. We will head to the woods. They will have to search the barn before they can come after us. By that time, the cavalry will have arrived." He hoped.

They headed toward the treeline at a rapid pace until Braeden stopped and dropped to the ground, pulling Jordyn down with him. They had been using the fence for cover and Braeden was glad that they had. Otherwise, the man standing in the trees would have noticed them before now. As it was, the glow of his cigarette was the only thing that saved their lives. "Thank you, Lord for his nasty habit," he said silently.

Braeden pointed him out to Jordyn and placed a finger over her mouth, indicating that she shouldn't talk. He lay there trying to decide what to do next. He was sure he could shoot the man, but he didn't really want to and he had no way of knowing there was only one man there. He had a feeling they were boxed in. He glanced at the barn and saw a light sweep the inside. As soon as they had finished searching the barn, they would know that they had headed this way.

He lifted his head and saw that the fence came within fifteen feet of the pool house. He leaned close to Jordyn's ear. "Is the back door to the pool house locked?"

He felt her shake her head and was glad that the night was cloudy. If he couldn't see Jordyn then the bad guys couldn't see them. He turned onto his back and handed Jordyn a small pistol that he pulled from his pants. "It's got six shots. Use it if you have to."

He felt her hand close over the gun and he gave it a squeeze before he released it. They began to crawl the distance from the field to the pool house. From there, Braeden didn't know what to do. They would have everything covered, the vehicles, the buggies. He wasn't sure how much time had passed but he was certain that Monica and her cronies should have been here by now. He checked his cell phone, concealing the glow as he did. There was no signal. He tried again a few feet later. Still no signal. That was odd. He frowned at his cell phone. He had made a call to Brock from the field only a few days ago and had good service. Suddenly, it dawned on him that along with cutting the phone lines, today's criminals had the ability to jam cell phone reception. It was up to him to get them to safety. He glanced back to check on Jordyn, crawling on the ground was not a forgiving past-time. She was right behind him though.

A hundred feet more had them directly across from the pool house door. However, the fifteen feet from the fence where they now lay to the door was exposed. Worse, they would have to crawl under the fence before they could run for it. Those seconds on the ground and in the open could prove deadly. A flashlight flickering over the field pushed him forward. He indicated that Jordyn should go first so he could cover in case someone spotted her. Without hesitation, she scooted under the fence and made it to the door with hardly any sound. Braeden followed as soon as she was inside. Despite himself, he felt his heart thump harder because he couldn't help but expect bullets to tear into his back before he made it to the door.

He closed the door softly, expecting to find Jordyn waiting just within. When she wasn't there he called softly. There was no reply. He had never been in the cavernous building and didn't know his way around. As he stepped toward the sound of sloshing water, a sixth sense warned him to duck. He still caught a glancing blow on the head and as he was falling to the ground, he had the sickening realization why Jordyn had not answered him.

Jordyn would have cried out at the dull thud of something hitting Braeden's head if a hand hadn't been covering her mouth. She had slipped into the door and stepped directly into the waiting arms of her captors. She could see enough to discern two shadows in the darkness. She had tried to warn Braeden only to be told if she didn't be still, they would shoot him. As the second man dragged Braeden from the changing room toward the pool, Jordyn tried desperately to think of a way to get free.

"Where are the lights?" The voice was accented but understandable and surprisingly smooth. The hand fell away from her mouth and she responded a bit shakily. "Beside the door."

She heard some movement and then blinked as light flooded the pool house. She looked around for Braeden and found him lying on the floor, apparently unconscious. "He doesn't look so pretty now, does he?"

Jordyn turned to the voice and was surprised to see Henry Lee. His smug face made her angry. She swallowed her fear for Braeden's life and sneered at the man. "Do you find it interesting that ugly, cowardly men always try to bring better men down to their level?"

Henry Lee's face went white with fury but he still smiled coldly at her. "You are going to die tonight, Ms. Grey. Depending on your attitude, you can die a long, hard death or very quickly." While still smiling at her, he kicked Braeden in the side. Braeden was slowly coming to and he moaned.

Jordyn watched as the man kicked Braeden twice more and felt like tearing into him. At that moment, Jordyn almost hated Henry Lee and he saw it in her eyes. "Poor, Ms. Grey," he said in false sympathy, "the men in her life keep getting in my way." He kicked Braeden again and he rolled away, knees pulled to his chest.

"What do you want?" Jordyn asked through clenched teeth, face pale with fury and fear.

"That's better," the man said as he walked toward Jordyn. "Cooperation is what I want, but I think you're still playing games with me." He leveled his gaze on her. "I think you know exactly what I want."

"The FBI and I have looked all over the place for the card. Don't you think I would have already given it to them if I had it or knew where it was?" Oddly enough, what Lee sought was still in the locker, not twenty feet from where he stood.

Henry Lee's laugh was one of the most evil things Jordyn had ever heard. She studied his face and wondered at him. The scar that ran from the corner of his left eyebrow to his chin made him look savage. It was jagged and purple. His eyes were almost merry with having her and Braeden at his mercy. He clearly delighted in kicking Braeden while he was helpless. Without having to be told, Jordyn knew that he was a being of concentrated evil. As he walked closer, she was desperately trying to tamp down the panic. For no reason Jordyn could explain, the name Jehovah-shammah came to mind. God is there. She remembered Pastor Charles' words about God being there no matter what you were going through. A peace settled on her that was not of this world. Henry Lee sensed it. Nothing could have given Jordyn more control of the situation than to take away his glee in her fear.

She met his eyes calmly. "It's not the card you want, is it? You want to feel safe and you can't. You can't feel safe because of all you have done. I'd say you can't even remember all of your evil deeds." Jordyn shook her head in genuine pity. "You won't find what you're looking for here."

Henry Lee clearly didn't believe her but neither did he know what to do. She wasn't frightened of him anymore. That he didn't understand.

While Henry Lee was contemplating what to do, all eyes were on him. There were four men, including Lee. Two were on the other side of the pool. The one holding Jordyn had let his grip loosen. Fortunately for her, they hadn't bothered to search her and she still had Braeden's gun tucked into her waistband beneath her shirt. Her eyes fell to Braeden. She was shocked to find him looking at her. He winked. Jordyn almost smiled. At her look, Henry Lee glanced at Braeden. He was still on the floor and his eyes were closed again.

"Your bodyguard wasn't much good."

Jordyn shook her head. "He's not my bodyguard. He's a wildlife biologist here on a research project."

Henry Lee smiled. The cold smile made fear slam into Jordyn's stomach again. Not for herself, but for Braeden.

Braeden saw that smile out of his narrowly opened eyes and knew what was coming. Every fiber of his being wanted to shut the man up. He would have happily strangled Lee if he could have gotten his hands on him.

"I'm afraid you were misinformed, my dear." The endearment grated on Jordyn. "Mr. Parker here has a brother who knew Tommy. Brock I believe his name is. Both Mr. Parkers appear to be employed by the US Marshals Service."

Jordyn's eyes flew to Braeden. He hadn't moved. "No." The word escaped softly, unbidden from Jordyn's lips.

Braeden was watching Jordyn's face. He felt sick. With those few words, Lee had destroyed every bit of her trust in Braeden. He should have told her when he had the chance. Now she would think everything in their relationship had been a facade. He decided that he might not be able to give her the truth but he would give her another chance at life. Even if it cost him his.

With Jordyn's shocked expression, Henry Lee had found a weak spot. He shook his head sadly. "I'm afraid so. I think he should be punished for the lie he's been leading, don't you?"

Henry Lee signaled the two men on the far side of the pool and they moved toward Braeden. As they got close, Braeden kicked one in the knee. The injured man fell to the ground with a cry and grabbed the blown knee. The second man was trying unsuccessfully to grab Braeden, who was on his feet and fighting for his life. The man holding Jordyn finally made the move Braeden had been waiting for. He let her go and moved to help his friend. He didn't want to tell her to run for fear of drawing attention to her departure. But rather than run as Braeden had expected, Jordyn yelled, "Get your hands off of him!"

Everyone stilled as they looked at Jordyn. She had the pistol Braeden had given her pointed right at Henry Lee's head. The man didn't look happy. "Which one of you didn't search her?"

The two that had been grappling with Braeden looked at the man holding his injured knee. Without warning, Henry Lee lifted his gun and shot the man. When he looked like he was about to move the gun toward Braeden, Jordyn said, "I wouldn't do that if I were you. I can't miss from here." Her voice was quiet and calm. Lee smirked, clearly not believing her, but not willing to risk it all yet.

Intensity came into her voice, surprising her as well as Braeden and their captors, but she had to make Lee believe. "If you think that I would hesitate for an instant, you would be betting your life on it. You killed my husband. Do you want to bet your life that I wouldn't be able to pull the trigger on the man that had Tommy killed?"

Braeden struggled back to his feet and disarmed and bound the other two men. He lined them up beside the pool and after securing their belts around their knees, he casually pushed them in. After regaining his breath and his feet, one of them sneered at Braeden. "You'll be dead before I'm dry."

Braeden ignored the man as he disarmed and bound Henry Lee. The man looked at him with pure hatred as Braeden shoved him into the pool. But he didn't say a word.

Braeden stared hard at Lee. "I'd say that after tonight no one is going to want to do anything for you. The FBI are on their way. That helicopter I'm hearing is theirs. You won't have anybody left who'll be willing to admit they know you by the time you stand trial." Braeden's eyes were flinty and Henry Lee recognized the truth of his words.

As Jordyn headed for the door, Braeden covered the men in the pool. They stepped outside to see vehicles with flashing lights heading toward the house and a helicopter with spotlights hovering over the house and barn.

Braeden reached for Jordyn's arm only to have her pull away. Her reaction made him cringe. "Jordyn." He made another grab for her arm. She stopped and turned.

The anger and betrayal in her eyes hit him like a physical blow. "*Don't touch me.*" Braeden let his hand fall, but still tried to explain.

Jordyn cut him off. "No! I don't want to hear one word. I don't want to hear from you or speak to you ever again. Do you understand me?" She was screaming by the time she finished. Braeden nodded and watched as she stormed away. The spotlight of the helicopter tracked her progress toward the house. He wanted to yell at them. He wanted to tell them all to go away. He wanted to run after Jordyn and make her listen. He wanted to tell her he loved her and that he wanted to marry her.

A flicker of movement in the barn loft caught his eye. He turned in time to see the laser as it pointed out the window. He knew it was aimed at Jordyn and he was too far away for an accurate pistol shot. Without caring for his own safety, he lifted the gun he'd taken from one of Lee's goons and began firing at the loft door as he ran toward the barn. The shot aimed at Jordyn found its mark and she went down. Anger and fear filled Braeden as he ran, firing as he went. He didn't remember doing it later, but when one gun was empty, he pulled the second gun he'd taken from the other goon and kept firing. He stopped twenty yards from the barn doors when the body of a man fell from the open loft and landed on the ground with a sickening thud.

Braeden ran toward Jordyn just as Monica and a team of medics made it to her. He started to kneel down next to her when he met her eyes. Jordyn stared at Braeden as the reality of all that had happened sunk in. Her eyes went to the gun in his hand. Everything passed in slow motion. He let the hand holding the one remaining gun relax, dropping it to the ground with a noise that sounded like thunder to him. He searched her eyes. The dread in his was matched only by the utter betrayal in hers. For a brief instant, he saw raw and bitter pain. Where he'd once seen his future, now he saw only anger. And then nothing. He took another step toward her only to stop at the look of absolute indifference. She held his gaze as people began to swarm everywhere at once. He heard his brother talking to him and felt him take his arm as he tried to lead him to a waiting ambulance. He saw Monica kneel next to Jordyn and take her hand. He stood rooted to the spot as Jordyn was hustled into an ambulance, blood soaking her shirt. He kept waiting for her to look around for him or for someone to call him to her. They didn't.

He told Brock where Lee was and a group of both FBI agents and US Marshals swept the pool area. They found Henry Lee and his henchmen on the floor of the pool house trying to loosen their bonds. Several others were arrested in the field as the helicopter turned small portions of the darkness into patches of broad daylight. Brock got a call from Monica and made his way to the pool house with a crime scene technician in tow. A little while later, they emerged with the card. So, Jordyn had figured out where the card was hidden. Braeden should have felt glad that the case was cinched and over as far as he was concerned, but as he sat in the ambulance waiting to be transported to the hospital, he found that he no longer cared about the case. All he cared about was the look in Jordyn's eyes. The horrific pain in his sides and chest with every breath didn't compare to the pain in his heart. He expected her to be angry over his deception, but the look in her eyes when they were taking her away made him think his worst fears had come true. He thought he may have lost Jordyn forever.

Against doctor's orders, Braeden made his way to the hospital the next day. He'd barely escaped a stay himself, having three cracked ribs and internal bruising from the brutal kicks of Henry Lee. He made it to the reception desk and was told that Jordyn Grey wasn't there. "She was brought in last night and treated for a gunshot wound. I know she hasn't been released yet."

The woman frowned at the man in front of her who looked like a brawler since Henry Lee and his men had gotten their hands on him and said, "I didn't say she had never been here. I said that she isn't here now."

"Where exactly is she?" He knew he sounded like a crazy man and he really didn't care.

It was clear that the nurse didn't want to talk to him, but the desperation in his eyes must have touched a chord because she said, "Her father checked her out this morning. I don't know where they went." Her tone implied that if she had known she wouldn't have told him.

Braeden was on his cell phone before he reached the doors. He almost ran smack into Brock on the way out. "She's not here, little brother."

Braeden glowered at him. "I know that."

"She doesn't have her cell phone either."

Braeden pulled his away from his ear. "Where's Monica?"

"They moved her to protective custody until we're sure that Henry Lee didn't know who she was."

Braeden stared at his brother in irritation. His ribs were killing him and his heart… "Are you going to help me find her?"

"She's in New York. Mr. Grey took her to be with her family."

"Did she leave a number?"

Brock shook his head. He didn't tell his brother that he had asked for a number. Jordyn's response had been less than kind.

"Did you see her?" When Brock nodded again Braeden asked, "How is she?"

"The doctor said that she'll be fine in a few months or so. The bullet didn't hit the bone. With rest, she'll make a full recovery."

Braeden swung his gaze from the parking lot to Brock. "That's not what I meant."

"She's understandably angry and hurt."

Braeden nodded. "I'll try to call her in a couple of days."

Brock didn't think that would be long enough, but he didn't say so. His brother had been through enough and he looked like he might fall at any second. "I'm proud of you, little brother." Braeden looked at Brock again, "You saved her life."

Braeden sighed. "I owed her. I should have told her the truth."

Brock didn't say anything. There was no response for that.

CHAPTER 22

Jordyn stared out at Washington, D.C., from her window. She had needed a place to escape to after it was all over and her father sent her to Washington. She was helping set up a branch office of the Grey Foundation there.

She sighed as they passed an electronics store. There was live coverage of Senator Booth's trial blurring through the rain-slicked window. The media had found out most of the story. They were covering the expedited trial of Senator Booth and they kept viewers abreast of what was happening with Henry Lee. Yes, they told the public everything they could find about her life and her marriage to Tommy. But they didn't know everything. There was no mention of Braeden except to say that someone with the US Marshal's Service had shot and killed the hired assassin who shot her, which wasn't exactly accurate. He actually wasn't a US Marshal. His law enforcement training from being a conservation police officer had been sufficient enough for Brock to convince his superiors that Braeden had adequate training for the undercover assignment. He'd saved her life. She should feel grateful for that and she did. But on the other hand, he'd stolen what little life she had made for herself by letting her fall in love with him when he'd only been there to help Brock.

He'd called constantly. The first few weeks he called numerous times every day. Her e-mail was flooded with pleas for her to call him. A month after she had left Promise Land, he'd left a message on her parent's voicemail telling her that he was going to stop calling, but when she was ready to hear his story to call him. Her mother and father had waited expectantly as she picked up the phone. They were disappointed when instead of greeting Braeden, she had blasted Monica for giving him her parent's private number. He hadn't called since.

The sleek, black limousine pulled up to her current home in Georgetown. Her father had rented the luxurious place for her. It was clear that he disagreed with her handling of Braeden but he didn't say anything. The house was beautiful and ritzy, glamorous and expensive, definitely not home. She longed for Tennessee and the tranquility of Promise Land but wasn't ready to face the memories.

She threw the jacket of her suit onto the table and longed for the everyday clothes of Promise Land. As she went to the kitchen and poured a mug of fresh, hot coffee, she reinforced her vow not to go back until Braeden was long gone. He'd be done with the wolf study by early May. She glanced at the calendar. Four weeks to go.

The phone rang and she answered, knowing without glancing at the caller ID who was going to be on the other end of the line. "Good evening, Mon."

"How'd you know it was me?"

Jordyn laughed a little at the surprise in Monica's question. "Because you've been calling me almost every evening for months to see if I'm going to call Braeden back."

"Well, are you?"

"No."

Monica sighed. "You're very stubborn."

"I know."

"And stupid."

The frustration and anger in Monica's voice shocked Jordyn. "Whoa, where'd that come from?"

Monica snorted her disgust into the phone. "You have a wonderful man who loves you and tried his best to keep you alive. He's tried to call you for months. He even called your Dad to plead his case. You have the chance of a lifetime. You have been blessed to love and be loved by two men and because the first one didn't live up to your expectations, you're not giving the second a decent chance."

"Thank you, Dr. Phil," Jordyn said sarcastically, something she had been more and more prone to of late.

"Fine. Make fun of me, that doesn't bother me and you know it. But Jordyn, don't ignore my advice. Grab him and don't let him go. Accept love again."

"Monica, he lied to me. He lied to me for months."

"No, he didn't. He just couldn't tell you the whole truth."

"A lie of omission is still a lie."

Monica ground her teeth together. "You don't get it. Don't you think he tried to tell you? He was going to tell you the night of the cleanup and a hundred times after that. He'd been planning to tell you a hundred times before that. Can't you get that he was so afraid of losing you that he couldn't tell you?"

"If we had what I thought we had, then he should have been honest with me earlier."

"Jordyn, can I ask something?"

"Since when do you ask before you bombard me with your opinions and questions."

"I'm going to ignore that and ask anyway. Why did you forgive me and not him?"

Jordyn didn't have an answer for that.

"We've been friends for years, but I never told you that I moonlight for the FBI. I was trying to get information out of you too. Why haven't you been so mad at me? In reality, mine was the worst betrayal because I was already your friend. Why not be mad at me?" Jordyn's silence lasted longer than a minute before Monica continued, "I'll tell you why. Because you love Braeden Parker and that scares you. You kept expecting him to do something wrong so you could curl back up into your shell and live safely and alone." Monica knew she was hurting Jordyn, but she was desperate. "Well, that's not fair to him or you. He loves you and whether he was right or wrong, he did what he did to protect you and your love for him. He asked your dad for your hand in marriage, did you know that? He loves you. Don't throw that away because you're too much of a coward to take a chance on love again."

The click in her ear made Monica wonder if she had pushed too far.

Jordyn felt the tears trickle down her face as she sat in the plush couch. She hadn't known he'd asked her dad if he could marry her. It was so sweet and old fashioned. Why couldn't he have just been honest with her? So what if he was afraid of losing her. That was no excuse not to tell her the truth because a relationship built on a lie was itself a lie. She had enough of that with Tommy.

No sooner had the thought formed than Jordyn realized that the truth worked both ways. Why hadn't she told him she loved him? If she were honest, it was because she was afraid of losing him. She didn't want to risk her heart on anything less than a certainty.

She spent a long, tearful night in prayer. She had a lot of things to apologize for. She also needed God's direction on how to fix the mess she had made of her life. The next morning, she had decided what she should do.

CHAPTER 23

Braeden drove the buggy through the gate to the backfield and glimpsed a tiny fawn standing in the small roadway. It was young and wobbly and downright adorable. Without thinking about it he turned to point it out to Jordyn and the smile on his face died. She wasn't there. He shook his head at himself. Seven months and it still hadn't sunk in that she was gone. He'd been completely unable to contact her. She didn't return the calls to the number he'd finally conned out of Monica. A few days after his last call, he'd received a card expressing the gratitude of the Grey family along with an offer of monetary support for any of his endeavors. It was signed by Jordyn. He'd lost his temper at the spitefulness of that note and had torn it up and mailed it back. There'd been no contact since. He'd heard that she had taken over the new offices of the Grey Foundation in Washington. There'd been a brief news bite on it as a sidebar to the trials. A news crew had caught her going into the new shiny building. He hadn't recognized the woman with the cold eyes and wearing an expensive business suit with every hair in place. He missed the braid with the wisps that had escaped into her eyes, begging to be brushed back. He missed the girl who sat beside him and played with red wolf pups with the delight of a child. He missed their dinners. He missed discussing his work with her. He missed their silly banter. He missed reaching over and holding her hand when driving over the land. He just plain missed her.

He wasn't so sure he'd really known her anymore though. She had been calm and reserved when she told the news crew she would be happy to comment on the new offices and only the new offices. A pushy reporter had asked if her gunshot wound had affected her work. Jordyn hadn't answered her. The woman finally asked a question about the new offices. Jordyn had responded to that question and seemed so in control of her life that Braeden felt slightly foolish for worrying about her. After her comments, they hadn't even attempted to follow her inside. There was something about her now that encouraged distance. He hated that. He hated that it was his fault. As he aimed the buggy for its usual parking place in the shed attached to the barn, he couldn't help but reflect on the fact that you always hurt the ones you love the most.

As he walked into the barn, he was surprised to find Brock sitting at one of the many tables in the war room, looking over the pictures on the table. There were stacks of pictures he'd gotten printed off. Any picture that had a wolf completely in the frame was printed. As he got closer, he noticed that Brock was studying the pictures at the bottom of the pile. They were of Jordyn. Or him and Jordyn. They hadn't been sure if one of the cameras was working properly so they had run back and forth in front of it trying to trip the sensor. They'd stood side by side and waved. Nothing had happened. Finally, as they had turned to one another and laughed at their failed attempts, the camera had flashed. It had taken a ton of pictures without flashing though and Braeden was glad that it had. They were the only pictures he had of the Jordyn he knew and loved.

"Hello, little brother," Brock said without looking up.

Braeden shook his head. He hadn't made a sound. "How do you do that?"

"It comes with practice." Brock smiled over his shoulder. "And you stink."

Braeden glanced down at the spot on his pant leg where he'd spilled some of his famous wolf lure. The smile died as a picture of Jordyn, nose scrunched in offense at the foul smelling concoction, flashed into his mind's eye. He sighed. "I had a spill."

"So I see. And smell." Brock slid off of the table and handed him the pictures. "How're you doing?"

Good ol' Brock. Honest and to the point. "Is that what you came all the way here to ask me?" Braeden took the pictures and stuffed them into a nearby briefcase.

"Yes," Brock's simple answer made Braeden stop and look his brother square in the eye. Brock was three years older and Braeden had always longed to be as tall as his brother. He'd finally caught up with him at around eighteen. He now met his brother eye to eye.

"I'm okay," he said with a shrug.

"Liar," the quiet challenge didn't surprise him. They'd been doing this since Braeden was in high school. Braeden wouldn't want to talk, saying he was fine. Brock would call him on it and force Braeden to open up and work through whatever had happened.

"I know. But if I keep saying it, it might eventually make it true."

Brock nodded and changed tactics. "Hungry?"

"Not really but I hear food is necessary for life. What are ya cookin'?"

Brock grinned. His cooking ability, or lack thereof, was well known in the family. The problem was that he loved trying to cook. "Chinese."

"Good, they deliver." Braeden ducked on his way out the door, instinctively knowing that his brother would send something flying at his back.

Later that evening, after polishing off enough delivered food for four people, the brothers found themselves watching the sunset from the fence attached to the barn and stretching down the path. They sat quietly enjoying the view, completely unaware of the picture they themselves made. A fiery gold and pink illuminated a rugged, mountain background. Partially blocking the panoramic view was the wide shoulders of two men sitting side beside, boots hooked on the bottom rail, hands braced at their sides on the top rail.

"You should talk to her," Brock said without preamble.

Braeden smacked his forehead. "Why didn't I think of that?"

Brock stared hard at Braeden. His little brother wasn't normally sarcastic, but he kept silent.

Braeden sighed. "I'm sorry, Brock. I'm just a bit cranky of late." He was quiet for a minute and then went on. "I did try to call her. For a month actually. She never called me back. She never answered my e-mail. I did get a card trying to give me money for saving her life." The bitterness in his voice at the memory made Brock more than a little angry at Jordyn. Braeden shrugged. "It's over."

"I'm sorry, little brother." The genuine regret in Brock's voice brought Braeden's head around.

"It's not your fault."

"In a way, it is. I asked for your help."

"But I could've told her the truth earlier if I hadn't been so afraid of losing her,"

Braeden turned his eyes back to the pink sky. "I lost her anyway though, didn't I." It wasn't a question.

"You were keeping quiet which is what I told you to do."

"That's a nice excuse to give me, but we both know I should've been honest with her."

Brock didn't answer for a while. He decided to push a little. "You didn't learn your lesson that well did you?"

Braeden frowned. "What do you mean?"

"Are you being honest now? You love her, Braeden. You're miserable. And from what I understand, so is she."

Braeden gave a short laugh. "I'll give you that I'm miserable and that I love her, but she didn't look so bad on the news the other night."

"From what you told me, that's not the girl you know. I don't think the girl you told me about would be happy living a life wrapped in a suit in Washington, D.C."

Brock jumped down from the fence and looked up at Braeden. "When you feel that the time is right, just be honest with her. Give your love a chance." He headed back toward the barn and Braeden's apartment.

Braeden sat on the fence for a while after the last vestiges of sunlight were long gone. He walked to the house. Once a week, Ava aired and cleaned it. He hadn't been back inside since the night of their desperate escape from the house. As he looked at the steps, he remembered Patrick Grey's plea and added failing him to his list of errors.

He walked around to the back patio and sat down in the seat he'd sat in for his first dinner with Jordyn. He remembered every expression, every gesture just as clearly as if it had just happened. He remembered how badly he'd wanted to protect her and take away her pain. He'd failed at that. Brock had good intentions with his advice, but Braeden felt that he had caused Jordyn enough pain. He'd be leaving in a few days. It was better that way. He was practically done with his research, but he'd been trying to hang around because he felt closer to Jordyn at Promise Land. Brock's words about love were beautiful but instead of encouraging him all they did was remind Braeden of what he'd lost. "And you lost big time," he said softly to himself. His only consolation was that Dave, Corey, and Neal didn't seem to hold anything against him.

CHAPTER 24

Jordyn felt like cheering. She was exhausted but happy. She was heading back to Promise Land. And she was heading back two weeks early. She had decided to talk to Braeden. She wasn't sure if a relationship between the two of them was possible, but she was giving herself two weeks to find out. She at least owed him the chance to explain, she knew that now. And she owed him an apology for not realizing that sooner. As she packed the last of her things, she couldn't help but smile at her own excitement. Not just over going home, but over seeing Braeden again as well.

As she pulled up to the house, she saw Dave heading her way. She was shocked at the tears that pricked her eyes at the sight of his familiar face. He helped from the car and pulled her into a tight hug. Unexpected tears blurred Jordyn's vision.

"Hi," was all she managed.

Dave set her back long enough to see that she was an emotional wreck but in one piece. "We missed you, girl. And not one of us appreciates you sending us away when you needed us the most."

"I know." Jordyn's quiet acceptance of his reprimand made him do a double take of her pale face.

"Where is he?"

Jordyn didn't have to explain who she was talking about. Dave sighed. "He left two days ago." Dave paused before continuing, "Let me help get your bags in."

"You don't have to haul my bags in. I can do it." Jordyn insisted.

"I know you can, but we want to do something for you so let us." Dave grumbled. Jordyn finally noticed Corey and Neal standing a few feet away, waiting to lend a hand. She smiled at them and had to fight tears again.

Hours later, Jordyn sat on the couch in Promise Land and stared out the window. She'd tracked down Brock to discover that Braeden had indeed left two days ago. Brock had obligingly helped him pack up all of his gear. She asked for a phone number to reach him and Brock hadn't answered her.

"Please Brock, I know I've been insensitive toward him, but I really think we should talk." Jordyn reasoned.

Brock sighed. "I would like to help you but you've called a bit too late. He left for Africa this morning. He took over a research project for a colleague who turned up pregnant."

"Africa?" Jordyn said in amazement. Braeden really did have a cool job. "What's he doing in Africa?"

"It's a camera survey of the interaction between lions and cheetahs. He was excited about going." Brock paused for emphasis. "I think he needed the space."

"How long is he going to be gone?" Jordyn asked, almost expecting the reticent Brock not to answer.

"At least three months, maybe more. He should be back in time for the fall semester." Brock decided to give Jordyn a little bit of a break. "He can check his e-mail every week or so. You can try that. I do agree that the two of you need to talk."

"Thanks, Brock," Jordyn said sincerely.

After that conversation, she found herself sitting on her couch doing a lot of soul searching. Her mind went back to when she had first met Braeden. It went back even further to Tommy. She thought about it a long time and decided to wait to talk to

Braeden. She could jump on the next flight or she could e-mail him, but for some reason she felt like she should wait. She owed him an apology face to face, and that apology would go better if she did some self-maintenance first.

The next weeks found Jordyn busily working on Promise Land and doing a lot of soul searching. Dr. Hayes was there for her newt study and there was plenty of paperwork to catch up on. About five weeks after she got back, she received the paper Braeden had written about the red wolves of Promise Land. It was good. He'd been able to get some very interesting data and make some recommendations for the future. There was not even a personal note in the package though. He'd air mailed it from Africa.

A few days later, Dr. Hayes was talking to her about the newest problem with the newt study. She stopped and said, "Ms. Grey, I don't want to seem like I'm prying, but I thought you should have this." She handed Jordyn an envelope. "It had fallen behind the bureau in the bedroom. I'll talk to you tomorrow."

Jordyn thought it odd behavior as she watched the small woman walk toward the barns. She pulled the flap open and looked inside. She pulled out a handful of pictures. The first one showed her waving her arms. The second showed her and Braeden standing side by side and waving furiously at the camera. The last shot had them smiling at one another. Jordyn didn't realize she was crying until the tears were dropping onto the picture. She wondered if he'd intended to leave them for her or simply lost them. Either way he had printed them and kept them in the envelope. She sighed as she settled into her porch swing. She missed him. She missed him a lot. As she sniffed in self-pity, she realized that no matter how long they were apart or how far away he was, she still loved him. That realization made her cry all the harder. She felt like her heart was going to shatter. But how could it when it was already in pieces?

Two days after seeing the pictures, Jordyn found herself in Pastor Charles and Ann's house. She sat in their living room having enjoyed a tall glass of "the best lemonade this side of anywhere." The peace that surrounded her longtime pastor and his wife was more comforting to Jordyn than she could ever explain. The early evening sun was turning anything it touched to a beautiful golden color that looked warm and clean and comforting. Jordyn was about to back out of talking to them when Ann smiled sweetly and said, "As much as we enjoy talking with you Jordyn, I feel that you didn't come here just for a chat. Is there anything in particular you would like to talk about?"

With those kind words, the floodgates opened and Jordyn found herself telling them her whole sorry story. She left out nothing and when she was done she felt relieved but way off kilter. She studied the solemn faces in front of her and tried not to feel as embarrassed as she knew she should be. Pastor Charles and Ann watched her without comment, waiting for her to finish.

"When I found out what he had done, I couldn't believe it. Once again, I had fallen for a man who had nothing but secrets. I'm not even sure that he genuinely cared for me at all." She sniffed a little and hated the way her statement sounded, so loaded with self-pity.

Ann cleared her throat. "First of all, have you forgiven God for not stopping you from marrying Tommy?"

"Yes," Jordyn's answer was simple but had a lot of meaning. She had been able to finally see that it wasn't God's fault, but the evil in the world that had caused the damage in her marriage. The beauty of salvation was that it was a commitment of free choice. God didn't force it on anybody. Tommy made his choices and she had chosen Tommy. And his murderers had made their choices.

"Have you forgiven God for letting you fall for Braeden?" The question was asked quietly, but pointedly.

Jordyn considered that question carefully before shaking her head. "I don't think I blamed God for Braeden's deceit. I mean, Braeden was the one who chose not to be totally honest with me.

So I guess the answer would be that I don't blame God for any of it."

"Do you blame Braeden for his choices?" Pastor Charles interjected.

"Well, not totally. He should have been honest with me upfront, but I understand why he wasn't. He had some fairly powerful people breathing down his neck. I am mad that once our relationship developed into something I thought could be permanent, he didn't tell me the truth." Jordyn stood and began to pace as she talked. "How hard is it to say, 'Honey, I'm working for the US Marshal's Service to try and catch your late husband's killer?' But he didn't even tell me before asking my father if he could marry me! What could he have been thinking?"

Ann nodded in understanding and Jordyn sat back down with a sigh. Pastor Charles leaned forward. "I need to ask you a question that may seem hard to answer, but I think you need to think about it before answering. Can you do that?" At Jordyn's nod he continued, "Are you hurt because Braeden lied or are you hurt because you fell for him?"

Jordyn had already opened her mouth to say no when she stopped to consider all of the repercussions of that question. Braeden had lied and that fact did hurt. But was her pride involved? Was she angry because her heart had been fooled into believing Braeden was nothing short of wonderful? He was wonderful, but was she angry that he wasn't perfect? So he had a secret—a large, gigantic, gargantuan secret—but did that mean he was any less than what she had thought him to be in the first place? Jordyn's confusion was plainly written all over her face and her frustration was apparent in the clenching of her hands.

Pastor Charles leaned forward and patted her hands. "You're not mad at God this time. Why? Because you recognize free choice. You're angry at Braeden for lying, but you seem to understand why he did it under the circumstances. Understanding isn't that far from forgiveness. So who are you really mad at and why?"

Jordyn sucked in her breath at the truth about to be exposed by his questions. "I'm mad at myself for falling for him in the first place, aren't I?"

Ann smiled and asked, "Are you? I have no doubt that you were bitter and angry at God over Tommy. But who did you really blame? Who have you not forgiven?"

"You mean besides the senator and company?" Jordyn's attempt at humor fell flat. They weren't letting her out of this one. She sighed heavily and admitted. "I guess I blame myself to a certain extent."

Pastor Charles looked at her steadily before saying, "You don't blame God anymore. You only partially blame Braeden. Why do you blame yourself?"

Jordyn thought a moment before finally coming totally clean. "I messed up with Tommy. I didn't go about dating or marriage in the right way and I know that. I knew that at the time, but I...I just wanted to be happy and I thought marrying Tommy would accomplish that. Braeden pointed out once that instead of blaming God, I should consider that maybe I was Tommy's chance at something personal with God and I see that, but I still made a mistake." After a long pause Jordyn went on, "I feel like I made the same mistakes with Braeden. I was only looking out for what I wanted, not what I needed."

"Why do you feel like falling for Braeden was a mistake?" Ann asked gently.

"Isn't it obvious? Our relationship is already sunk because of all of the baggage."

Pastor Charles asked, "Was falling for Tommy a mistake?"

"Not entirely, I can see that now."

"Then what makes you think that you messed things up with Braeden. No relationship is perfect. A perfect marriage is one constantly under construction. Sometimes you mess up and have to patch a hole or knock out a wall, but it keeps getting better."

Jordyn studied the couple sitting side by side, hand in hand. They knew what they were talking about and it showed. Could there still be a chance for her and Braeden?

"So you think Braeden and I have a chance at a marriage like yours?" Jordyn asked doubtfully.

Ann nodded. "Yes, but only if you're able to work on it."

Jordyn laughed without much humor and said wryly, "That's a little hard to do when he's a world away."

"Well, then I guess you need to start working on you now so that when he gets back you'll be ready to tackle your foundation."

Jordyn stared her eyes moving comically from one to the other in complete confusion. "What exactly does that mean?"

Pastor Charles took over. "Before you can consider a relationship with someone else, romantic or otherwise, you need to make sure you're relationship with God is in good working order. You need to talk to him every day, read his instruction manual, and be ready to accept what he says."

"I've been working on that," Jordyn admitted.

"Good. Keep at it. You'll need him more than ever as you start to work on yourself. You've got to forgive yourself and learn to trust yourself before you can completely trust your heart to someone else." Pastor Charles said this and smiled. "And believe me it's a lot harder than it sounds."

"But Pastor Charles and I have no doubt that you can do it," Ann said as leaned over to pat Jordyn's hand lying on the arms of her rocking chair.

Jordyn nodded. "I think I can do that."

"That's not all." Pastor Charles looked down at his shiny black shoes before adding, "You also have to forgive Braeden completely and decide if you can trust him enough to be the head of your house."

Jordyn sighed. "This is going to be physically and emotionally draining, isn't it?"

Both Pastor Charles and Ann laughed at Jordyn's tone and expression. Ann smiled encouragingly at Jordyn. "Yes, sweetheart, but it will be worth it. And we'll be there every step of the way."

Jordyn was never surer of that than when she left that evening after an excellent home-cooked meal and a personalized week of Bible study Pastor Charles had made just for her.

Jordyn might have been surprised to find that Braeden was doing much the same thing she was…only in a hotter locale. The same day Jordyn talked to Pastor Charles and Ann found Braeden in his small room staring at a picture he'd made Brock send him that had arrived that day. He'd really blown it with her. How could he have been so blind? How could he have risked losing her? He swallowed hard as he thought about how he could call himself a Christian after deceiving her like he did. He knew his reasons were pure in the beginning but toward the end, he hadn't told her because he was afraid of losing her.

He flung the envelope on the floor and some paper fell out. Retrieving it Braeden found that it was a letter from Brock.

Hey Bro,

I know letters are a bit traditional in the modern day of e-mail, but I thought you might be more receptive of what I have to say with that picture in your hand. Don't shake your head, I know you didn't put it down just to read a letter.

I wanted to tell you that I'm sorry for getting you involved in my problems. I shouldn't have pushed you to do something I knew went against your grain. I'm well aware that I might have cost you more than I can ever make up for. All I can do is ask for your forgiveness and tell you that if you need anything, I'm there.

Lastly, I want to tell you to think long and hard before you write off a chance of a relationship with Jordyn. Trust me, women don't get that mad without a whole lot of feelings being involved. Your pastor sent along a sheet of paper with some Scriptures on it (Yes, I talked to him. He's my pastor too). He said before you can talk to Jordyn, you need to have a long talk with God about yourself. Anyway, I look forward to seeing you when you get home. Take care, little brother. I would hate to explain to mom how you got eaten by a lion.

Brock

Braeden read the letter twice before looking at the sheet of paper his pastor had sent. It was Scriptures all right. Rather than be angry at Brock, he was beginning to see the truth in his words. No matter how his relationship with Jordyn turned out, he would need to face her and apologize. But not before he got forgiveness from God and himself. The evening sounds of the bush found Braeden kneeling in prayer.

CHAPTER 25

In return for all of their hard work and since she hadn't hosted a summer's end picnic for her church last year, she decided to throw a huge Fourth of July picnic. She seriously thought the entire town showed up. Monica and Faith were there with their families and most of the church.

Pastor Charles and Ann smiled lovingly at Jordyn as she meandered up to the porch swing. "How's your day been, dear?" Ann asked.

Jordyn smiled with genuine warmth. It was amazing the change the last few months had brought. "I'm having an almost idyllic day. But I will admit to being slightly weary right now."

"Well, you see who is taking shelter on your front porch," Pastor Charles joked. "I think we're getting too old to party all day."

"Oh posh," Jordyn scolded. "You'll never be too old for that."

"Have you talked to your young man yet?"

Jordyn met Ann's question in the candor with which it had been asked. It had become a common question over the last few months. She had sat in their cozy home and told them her whole story, from the day she met Tommy on. They had listened to her anger, self-recrimination, and woes of love with loving concern and Godly advice. She finally felt that she could tell Braeden she forgave him for his deceit and apologize for her own transgressions. And she intended to do it in person. "No, Brock said he'd be back sometime in July. I guess I'll hear from Brock whenever Braeden makes it back. If he's not going to come to me then I guess I'll have to make the first step."

They both nodded seriously but Jordyn thought she saw a twinkle of amusement in Ann's eye. When Ann noticed her look she smiled and said, "It's so nice to see young love."

"That it is," agreed Pastor Charles.

"Well, I don't know that I would be so optimistic about it yet," Jordyn cautioned.

"Oh, I have a good feeling about your young man," Ann said with a mischievous smile.

After a few more minutes laughing and enjoying the festivities with her pastor and his wife, they shooed her off of the porch. "Go enjoy your other guests. You don't have to stay here with us."

Jordyn secretly thought that they were enjoying sitting on the porch and watching their people bustle about, so she left the porch to wander the festivities. Jordyn had arranged a trap shoot and was pleasantly surprised when Luke Stettleman won. She was even more surprised to see Monica cheering louder than anyone else. She must have really been out of it not to notice that Monica might have jumped into the uncharted waters of romance. The volleyball courts were well-populated and the tennis courts didn't lack for exuberant players either. There was a line to play horse shoes and a line for the roasted corn. All in all, Jordyn thought the party a success. She couldn't wait until the fireworks and marshmallow roast.

"It's a great party. Thanks for inviting us." The voice came from behind Jordyn and she turned with a ready smile. She hadn't known for sure if he would come. She hadn't been prepared for how Brock's smiling face reminded her enough of Braeden's to bring a pang.

"You're welcome. I'm glad you could all come. It was the least I could do after all you've done." Jordyn's smile held a sincere warmth that Brock noticed and was immensely glad for. While trying to invite some of the key people in her case to the party, she had spoken with Brock often the past couple of weeks. Even though she thought he was finally getting warmer toward her, he still hedged around giving her a date for Braeden's return home. She couldn't blame him for that though and refrained from asking him about it now.

He suddenly looked uncomfortable as he said, "Well, I'm going to go try my hand at horse shoes."

As she watched him walk away, Patrick Grey ambled over from the pool house and gave his daughter a sideways hug. "I'm glad you decided to do this."

Jordyn smiled and hugged him back. "Thanks, Dad. I'm glad I did too, but I will admit, I'm pretty beat."

"Why don't you take off for a little while before supper starts? Dave has Gravity saddled for you."

"I'm surprised at that. He hasn't been talking to me much since he realized I sent him and the guys to fix the campground up, in order to get them out of the way. He thinks they should have been here to help me." She smiled as she remembered how often Braeden's praises had been sung in her earshot when she had returned home. Apparently, Braeden's heroism in saving her life had won him Dave's undying support.

Patrick smiled down at his daughter. "Take a ride down to the pond and relax a little. Maybe you can catch a nap before you have to come back and play hostess."

Jordyn looked at her father in surprise. "How did you know that's just what I needed?"

"Because I'm your daddy and it's my job to know." He smiled smugly at her. "Head down to the big pond. It's amazing the peace of mind one can get from a visit there. I'm pretty sure no one is fishing at the big one right now."

"And how would you know that," Jordyn asked skeptically.

"Because it's too hot for fish to be biting much right now. Besides," he said with a grin, "I've been directing everybody to the south pond." He looked so satisfied with himself that Jordyn had to laugh.

She made her way toward the barn, speaking to a few people along the way. She couldn't help but feel appreciative of how monetarily blessed she was. She had determined weeks ago to figure out how to give more. This party was the first step toward that goal.

As she approached the barn, she was surprised to hear Neal's voice saying, "That's all there is to it. Just ask him to forgive and live in your heart. He'll be there for you no matter what."

A young voice asked, "Do I have to do it right now?"

"No, you can do it anytime, anywhere. God always hears. All you have to do is trust in him."

Jordyn felt tears drip from her chin before she even knew she was crying. She could still remember the angry face of the boy Dave gave extra chores to. She remembered the Neal who had disliked Braeden on sight and made no apology for it. Wouldn't Braeden like to see him now, witnessing and everything? As she had worked on her spiritual foundation, she had found herself more inclined to help Dave with Neal and their efforts had paid off.

Jordyn waited in the quiet stillness of the barn for Neal to finish talking to the boy. After praying with him for a few minutes and then talking a bit more, the little fellow ran off to find his mom and tell her about his salvation.

Jordyn stepped from the cool shadows and smiled at Neal who was absolutely beaming. "You did good."

"You were here the whole time?" Neal asked.

"No, I came up right before he prayed. I've never been more proud of you." Jordyn's voice and smile said it all.

"Yeah, well. It's a lot better feeling than anything I used to be up to." Neal absently drew random designs in the dry dirt of the barn floor before saying, "Dave said he's been thinking about hiring a permanent hand around here."

Jordyn frowned a little. "You don't want to go to college?"

Neal looked shy but sure of his words. "I do, but I want to stay here for a few years first." He met her eyes and the pleading she saw in his brought an instant response. "I'll still start college when I'm nineteen, but I want to be sure..." He let his words hang.

Jordyn nodded in understanding. "You have a home here for as long as you feel you need it." Feeling that the boy might need more assurance she added, "It'll be nice to have someone younger around to help Dave and Corey." She shot him a quick grin. "But don't you dare tell either of them I said that."

"Oh, I won't. I wouldn't want Dave proving that he's still stronger than I am."

"We definitely can't have that," Jordyn said with a light laugh. "Dad said that I might have a horse saddled for me to make a little escape."

Neal grinned boyishly. "Per your Dad's instructions to Dave and Dave's to me. He told me earlier that the big pond shouldn't have anybody there."

"Well, that sounds like the perfect place to take a break before the fireworks."

"It would be a nice place to share." Neal's quietly spoken words made Jordyn's head whip around. She thought they'd overcome his infatuation.

Neal saw her surprise and quickly amended, "I wasn't suggesting with me." He shuffled a bit before he continued, "I just wanted to say I hope things between you and Braeden work out. If you want it to." His ears turned red as he finished. "He just seemed like a great guy."

Jordyn was truly touched. "Thank you, Neal. I guess all we can do is pray about it and leave it in God's hands." With that, Jordyn swung up on Gravity and headed out of the barn at a trot.

Neal stood staring after her. "You have no idea how much we've all been doing that."

In a few minutes, she and Gravity were heading out on the trail to the pond. She had been back several times since last year when she and Braeden had enjoyed their afternoon there. It had brought back pleasant thoughts instead of painful ones.

She let Gravity graze and headed toward the pond, enjoying its sparkling beauty in the afternoon light and its unique sounds. As she got closer to the gazebo, she realized that someone had obviously chosen to fish here instead of at the south pond. A lone fisherman was sitting on the dock, feet dangling in the water. She figured it was one of the guys slipping to a new hole for the biggest fish. She couldn't tell which because of the floppy fisherman's hat.

"Are they biting?" Jordyn asked cheerily as she headed toward the seated fisherman.

Her heart stuck in her throat when the fisherman swept off his hat and turned to smile at her.

"Braeden," she whispered, but he heard her.

"Hey, you," he said softly.

Jordyn stared at his beautiful, dear face. He was thinner. His hair had been streaked by the hot African sun, and she thought he looked a little tired…and wonderful.

"How was Africa?" She asked even though that was the last thing she wanted to talk about.

He smiled a lopsided, adorable grin. "Hot."

"It's been pretty warm here too." Jordyn was inwardly kicking herself. She loved this man dearly and had a ton of things to say and instead of saying them, she was calmly conversing about the weather.

Braeden smiled at Jordyn. He couldn't stop smiling at her. She looked good. Brock had said she had looked tired to him, but she must have rejuvenated. He sat for a few seconds longer and then couldn't wait any longer. He got up and headed toward her.

Jordyn watched as Braeden slowly put down his pole and stood. He moved toward her and about a foot away he stopped. She looked into his beautiful blue eyes and felt tears welling up in hers. She never knew who reached first but in the next instant she was in his arms and hugging him for all she was worth. "I've missed you."

Braeden smiled. He'd never heard her be so honest about her feelings. "I've missed you too."

Jordyn pulled back slightly. "I have a lot I need to tell you but I'm going to start with the important stuff. I'm sorry I was so angry with you. I should have given you a chance to explain and I'm sorry I didn't." She sighed heavily. "The truth is I was angrier at myself than you." She held up her hand to stall his words. "I know I was angry at you but believe me you were the scapegoat for a lot of it. I've had a lot of stuff to work through and what I've seen in myself wasn't so pretty. I should have handled the situation a lot differently. I think I lost someone very dear to me because I didn't give you a chance to explain and I'm very sorry for it…"

Braeden shook his head at her rapid flow of words, desperately hoping that the "someone dear" to her she thought she had lost was him. "I should have told you sooner. I've had to do some soul searching too. I can in no way justify lying to you. I need your forgiveness for that."

"You have that forgiveness, Braeden, as well as an apology for not talking to you about it."

"I didn't blame you for not wanting to talk to me. Under the circumstances, I didn't even want to talk to me." Jordyn smiled at the self-deprecating words. "We both made mistakes. It's over now though. As long as you're still my friend, I'll work from there."

Jordyn's face clouded and she pulled away from him. He resisted the urge to pull her right back where she belonged. "Is that all we are now, Braeden? Friends?"

"I hoped we could be more, but…" He let his words trail off.

Jordyn misunderstood the silence. She thought he was telling her that friends were all they could ever be. She shook her head. "Then I don't think we can even be friends, Braeden. My heart can't take that. You see, I didn't tell you this, but I love you. I've loved you for a long time and I've fought hard against it. Pastor Charles says I need to stop running away from things I fear and let God handle them. Well, I'm trying to do that. I'm not running away from my feelings, but neither can I just push them aside and pretend to be your bosom buddy. I can't do that. I love you too much to do that. And it's not funny." Jordyn practically shouted at him once she saw the smile nearly splitting his face.

Braeden had started to smile at her third sentence and was almost laughing by the end of her burst of words. He grabbed her to him and kissed her long and passionately.

He laughed as he let her go far enough to look at his face. He wanted her to see that he was serious. "I'm laughing because I love you too."

Jordyn put both hands on either side of his face and searched his eyes. "Are you sure?"

Braeden nodded and then leaned down to kiss the tears that had began to silently slip down her cheeks. "I love you more than I ever thought it was possible to love someone. I even ran away to Africa to escape it, but I carried it with me."

"Even though you didn't have your pictures?"

Braeden winced. "You found those, did you? I meant to take them with me but when I got there I couldn't find them. I got Brock to send me a copy. He called me a glutton for punishment, but it was worth it."

Jordyn smiled. "Good. Mine are streaked almost beyond recognition."

"I'm sadly thrilled over that," he said as he squeezed her tighter.

They stood in one another's arms for a while, neither wanting to let go. A thought occurred to Jordyn. "Braeden, did my Dad know you were out here?"

"Sweetheart, he sent me out here when Brock arrived with me in tow. I showed up when you were helping some little girl with a Band-Aid and he sent me out here with the promise he'd send you when he could." Braeden chuckled. "For a while I thought he was just trying to get rid of me until I heard your horse. I think your pastor and his wife were in on it too."

Jordyn sighed with contentment. "I think Neal might have known something as well." She made a mental note to tell Braeden about Neal's progress later. All she wanted to do right now was enjoy being in the arms of the man she loved unreservedly. "Remind me to thank them later. I'd go now but I don't want to let you go, and I wouldn't have any dignity left if everyone saw me hanging onto you like a drowning woman."

"Maybe not but I sure enjoy it."

They laughed softly, still standing in their embrace. Finally, Braeden pulled back. "I really do need to talk to you, Jordyn."

Jordyn sighed and pulled away reluctantly. She pulled her boots and socks off and sat down, feet dangling in the water. She was quite different than she was during that stupid interview. Braeden joined her, smiling at the picture she made despite the seriousness of their impending conversation.

He sighed. "I guess I need to start at the beginning. I really did plan to do a red wolf study here starting this past spring. I told Brock about it one day and he jumped at the chance to get me onto Promise Land early. I told you about being a conservation officer in college. My training was sufficient for Brock to arrange for me to come in under the US Marshal's Service. They'd been trying to nab Lee for a while and he thought you might be the best chance." He paused before going on. "For two weeks, I learned everything I possibly could about Tommy Michaels and Jordyn Grey. I read tons of newspaper clippings and magazine articles, not to mention files on both of you. Brock knew about my upcoming study and thought that I was the best shot at finding out if you knew anything while keeping a surreptitious eye on the place."

Jordyn listened as she swirled her feet in the cool water. Braeden lifted her chin with a finger. "I'm sorry."

"Go on," she said quietly.

"Well, needless to say, you weren't what I expected. After about two days, I wanted to tell you everything. But I was torn. If you didn't know anything then I wanted to keep it that way. You were safer. On the other hand, I desperately needed to know what you knew as soon as possible." Braeden's frustration at his dilemma was evident in the way he frowned at the memory of those days.

"So, the plan all along was for you to…woo me into telling you everything?" Jordyn couldn't help but trip over the words.

"No!" Braeden said emphatically. "There was not supposed to be anything like that. I was supposed to see if you knew anything and if so, exactly what you knew by working with you and developing a trust." He sighed heavily. "Please believe that I didn't set out to hurt you. I was honestly trying to protect you."

Jordyn looked at him. "You could have told me."

"I know that now. I should have told you a hundred times after the house break-in too. I just didn't want to lose you." He raised a hand to her face, gently cupping her jaw. "By that time, I was hopelessly head over heels for you."

Jordyn turned her eyes away, unable to stand the look of pain she found in his. "I should have been honest with you too. I should have contacted the authorities as soon as I got the first call. And I should have trusted myself and my judgment enough to confide in you." She shrugged. "We were both wrong."

Braeden leaned his forehead to touch hers. He was so relieved that she understood. He knew he had hurt her badly, but he intended to spend the rest of his life making up for it.

"Jordyn Grey, will you be my girl? Will you go on dates with me, take long rides, and eat pizza on the patio with me?"

Jordyn's heart slammed into her chest. For a split second, she had been afraid he was going to ask her to marry him. She didn't think they were ready for that. They needed time to get to know one another under normal circumstances.

"I'd like that," she said simply.

Braeden tilted his head down and sealed their new relationship with a kiss. He had a feeling he was going to like being Jordyn's boyfriend.

Jordyn couldn't help responding to his kiss with all of the love inside her. They may not have had a traditional courtship, but she already loved this man dearly. And she recognized the promise of forever in his kiss.

EPILOGUE

Three years later.

Braeden smiled at his wife as he walked in from a long day of looking after Promise Land. After their marriage two years ago, he had quit his job and took on running Promise Land full time so Jordyn could stay in charge of the Grey Foundation. He'd even added to the property. He'd become a popular and sought after speaker on wildlife conservation. He and Jordyn had traveled all over to hotspots in the world of conservation.

And that's not all they were up to. Brock frequently used a cabin on the backside of the property as a safe house for federal witnesses. As a matter of fact, he had told Braeden that he might be by tomorrow. After all that they had been through, Braeden and Jordyn felt they should do all they could to help others in serious danger. Three months ago, Jordyn had led a young woman to Christ who found herself married to an arms dealer.

As he was reflecting on how wonderful their life together was, he made it to the porch and pulled his wife into a bear hug, kissing her noisily. She laughed and tugged him onto the porch swing. "How was your day?'

Braeden extended his cut hands for his wife's inspection. "It was fine. Definitely busy, but the fences needed repaired."

"Oh, poor baby," Jordyn cooed and then smiled. "I'd say you left some sections in strategic locations in pitiful shape though."

Braeden shrugged innocently. "Well, it's nice to make it easier for the deer, wolves, and other critters to cross the fence."

Jordyn cocked her head to the side. "How many cameras did you set up over those spots?"

Braeden burst out laughing. "You know me too well."

"How many?" Jordyn insisted teasingly.

"Eighteen," Braeden said in a tone that greatly resembled a little boy caught sneaking a frog into the house.

"Well," Jordyn said blithely as she ran her fingers through his hair, "I hope you enjoy taking pictures of children as much as you do animals."

"And why would I need to do that?" Braeden asked distractedly, enjoying the attention.

When Jordyn didn't answer, Braeden looked at her. For the first time, he noticed how happy and content his wife looked. He suddenly understood.

"Are you…"

"Pregnant," Jordyn finished for him when his words trailed off.

A millisecond later, Jordyn found herself hauled onto his lap and thoroughly kissed. "I take it you're happy," Jordyn asked with a smile.

"I'm thrilled! I'm going to be a daddy." He looked into Jordyn's eyes. "Are you okay with this? It may interfere with your career for a while."

Jordyn smiled and wrapped her arms around her stomach. "I'm more than okay with it. I'm going to have the baby of the man I love. What's not wonderful about that?"

"In about eight months or so you might figure out something," Braeden said teasingly.

Jordyn smiled that special mysterious smile only an expectant mother has. "I'm sure it's worth it."

Braeden turned Jordyn's back to his chest and sat with his arms around her, hands lightly resting on her stomach. Jordyn found herself thinking back to the tumultuous days when she wasn't sure if they would ever be together. Jehovah-nissi. When Braden saw the smile he loved so well he asked, "Have I told you I love you today?"

"Yes, but you can say it again."

"I love you, Jordyn Parker," Braeden said softly in her ear.

"And I love you," Jordyn whispered back.

His lips found hers once again. They sat in the swing long into the evening, watching the sunset and planning their future with a prayer in their hearts for the new life they had created.

Lightning Source UK Ltd.
Milton Keynes UK
UKOW07f2203141214

243121UK00015B/185/P